Up in Smoke

Nick Brooks

May 2025

ADVANCE READER'S EDITION—NOT FOR SALE

PLEASE NOTE: This is an uncorrected proof. Reviewers are requested to check all quotations against the published edition. Price and publication date are subject to change without notice. For more information, please contact childrens.publicity@macmillanusa.com.

Perfect for fans of Karen McManus and *The Hate U Give*, this edge-of-your-seat thriller from the author of *Promise Boys* follows a girl determined to clear her brother's name and a boy desperate to keep his own out of the line of fire. As the heat turns up in a murder investigation, old feelings reignite between them, but a shocking secret could tear them apart.

After Cooper King is pressured by big-brother figure Jason to go on a looting spree during a local march, the unthinkable happens: Gunshots ring in the air and someone ends up *dead*. After Cooper flees, the news shows four teens in ski masks near the scene of the murder—Cooper and his friends. Cooper fears the cops will come knocking at his door, and the pressure only mounts when a suspect is taken into custody: Jason.

Monique, Jason's sister and Cooper's longtime crush, is willing to go any length to clear her brother's name. Even if she needs to go into the belly of the beast and confront the killer herself. When she teams up with Cooper, they fall down the investigation rabbit hole and start to fall for each other. But little does Monique know that within this web of deception, Cooper is shrouding the truth that he was there when the shots went off. If the pair fail to uncover the real murderer, Jason will get locked up for a crime he didn't commit—and drag down Cooper with him.

Nick Brooks is the critically acclaimed author of *Promise Boys* and award-winning filmmaker from Washington, DC. He is a 2020 graduate of USC's TV and film production program. His short film, *Hoop Dreamin'*, earned him the George Lucas Scholar Award and was a finalist in the Forbes 30 Under 30 Film Fest. Before becoming a filmmaker, Nick was an educator working with at-risk youth, and many of his stories are inspired by his experiences with the children and families of his community. He is also the author of the middle grade series Nothing Interesting Ever Happens to Ethan Fairmont. Follow Nick on X @whoisnickbrooks and on Instagram @officialnickbrooks. thenickbrooks.com

Marketing & Publicity Campaign

- Select Author Appearances
- Appearances and Promotions at Book Festivals and Conferences
- National YA and Consumer Media Campaign
- Major National Consumer and Trade Advertising Campaign
- Digital Influencer Campaign Targeting Young Adult and Thriller Online Tastemakers
- Fierce Reads Social Media Engagement Campaign
- Email Marketing Campaign Targeting Young Adult Subscribers
- Extensive E-Galley Distribution to Booksellers, Reviewers, Librarians, Educators, and Consumers
- Promotions on Netgalley and Edelweiss
- Extensive Outreach to Key Educators and Library Contacts
- A fiercereads Title—Visit Fiercereads.com to Learn More

Imprint Name
An Imprint of Macmillan
120 Broadway, New York, NY 10271
mackids.com

ISBN: 978-1-250-35993-3
Price: $19.99 US / $26.99 CAN
On Sale Date: 05/06/2025
Category: Young Adult Fiction
Format: Jacketed Trade Hardcover
Pages/Trim: 304 (est.) / 5-3/8" × 8-1/4"
Age: 14–18

UP IN SMOKE

Much love!

PRAISE FOR *PROMISE BOYS*

Odyssey Award for Excellence in Audiobook Production for Young Adults

Texas Library Association TAYSHAS Top Ten Book Selection

Amazon Best Book of the Year So Far

Boston Globe–Horn Book Award Honoree

New York Public Library & Kirkus Best Book of the Year

A Project LIT Community Book Club Pick

★ "A top-notch page-turner and deep character study . . . will grip readers, who won't want to stop reading."
—*Booklist*, **starred review**

★ "Breathtakingly complex and intriguing."
—*Kirkus Reviews*, **starred review**

★ "Brooks excels in creating protagonists worthy of applause and truly foul villains, whose presences linger long after this atmospheric read ends."
—*Publishers Weekly*, **starred review**

★ "This cinematic thriller deftly entertains readers while leveling a sharp indictment of society's mistreatment of Black and Latinx teenage boys. A tense and urgent mystery that can help break the cycle it condemns."
—*Shelf Awareness*, **starred review**

UP IN SMOKE

NICK BROOKS

HENRY HOLT AND COMPANY
NEW YORK

Henry Holt and Company, *Publishers since 1866*
Henry Holt® is a registered trademark of Macmillan Publishing Group, LLC
120 Broadway, New York, NY 10271 • mackids.com

Copyright © 2025 by Nick Brooks. All rights reserved.

Our books may be purchased in bulk for promotional, educational, or business use. Please contact your local bookseller or the Macmillan Corporate and Premium Sales Department at (800) 221-7945 ext. 5442 or by email at MacmillanSpecialMarkets@macmillan.com.

Library of Congress Cataloging-in-Publication Data is available.

First edition, 2025
Book design by Rich Deas
Printed in the United States of America

ISBN 978-1-250-35993-3 (hardcover)
1 3 5 7 9 10 8 6 4 2
10 9 8 7 6 5 4 3 2 1

[Dedication TK]

You can jail a revolutionary,
but you can't jail the revolution.
You can murder a liberator,
but you can't murder liberation.

—Fred Hampton

PART ONE
CHAOS

CHAPTER ONE
COOPER
TAX SEASON

"Yo! They finally hitting H Street!" Rico yelled, crashing through the door.

His T-shirt was drenched with sweat and his locs frizzy from the humidity in the air. The sun spilled in behind him, briefly illuminating Jason's dim basement where a couple other guys from the neighborhood were posted up. Everybody was frozen still, but I looked over to Jason to see how he'd respond. This was the news we'd all been waiting for, but I secretly hoped we wouldn't get.

"Bet. Let's move," Jason said, starting for the door. He jumped up so fast his head nearly hit the wobbly ceiling fan spinning for dear life. But he was either too high or too focused to notice.

I rose to my feet, but my stomach felt like it was still glued to the couch. A dribble of sweat crept down my forehead as I gripped my lucky bracelet. A nervous tic. I wasn't so much afraid of hitting the streets, but my father's words ringing in my head terrified me. *Don't go down to that protest, Coop. Or else . . .*

"You coming?" Jason called as the homies filed out of the small basement. "No pressure, li'l bro."

I knew he meant it, but I still didn't want to disappoint him. Jason was like my big brother. He looked out for me in ways I could never repay. No way I could get cold feet at the last minute.

"Hell yeah," I yelled back as I stepped out the door, exuding a confidence I didn't possess. Jason closed the door behind us and the click of the lock told me there was no turning back.

As soon as we got outside, the thick, dry summer air smacked me in the face. I could feel the beating sun melting away any nervousness I felt. DC was the hottest it's ever been. Literally. The summer had already broken multiple heat records and showed no signs of slowing down anytime soon.

But summer meant folks was outside. Outside meant trouble. And ever since the mayor announced the city cut jobs from SYEP, the Summer Youth Employment Program, DC had been a powder keg.

SYEP promised to employ kids ages fourteen to twenty-one all over the city as a way of keeping them off the streets. It was a program I had participated in since I was first eligible. But with it gone, the city felt like it was turning upside down. Every other week news channels went on and on about a shooting or a robbery or a carjacking, and DC's youth was always the culprit. I got the picture; crime was up.

But the part they didn't talk about was that people were struggling. It was like the city was squeezing tighter and tighter by the day and people were suffocating and my pops and I were no different. I'd planned my whole summer around the SYEP gig I was supposed to have, which was one of the reasons I was headed to H Street with the big homies.

This all started last weekend, the match that lit the fuse, when a kid named Samir was killed by a plainclothes cop. He was only fourteen, just a couple years younger than me. The craziest part was, I knew Samir. He went to my high school and lived around the way. He was a quiet kid, not even a troublemaker like that.

The shooting happened right down at Union Station, not far from where we lived. Allegedly, Samir snatched a purse from a white lady in the subway. He was running away, headed for the exit, when a bystander, the plain clothes, blasted him for no reason. They said he had a blicky on him, but it had to be all lies. Samir didn't pose a threat to nobody—he was just a kid.

To make matters worse, there had only been forty bucks in the purse. Two twenty-dollar bills in exchange for his young life.

People flipped. Not just Black ones neither. Any and everybody with eyes could see what was happening. They said if the city gave jobs back to the kids, they wouldn't have to rob and steal. *No shit*, I thought.

When the Metropolitan Police Department, or MPD, refused to arrest the man that pulled the trigger, the uproar began online. People posting slideshows and collages on their social media pages, of all the things they could get for forty dollars. The last slide was always a picture of Samir and underneath their post they'd use the hashtag: **#FORFORTYBUCKS**.

The woke types thought it was profound, but I personally thought the posts were a little sick. People who didn't even know Samir were posting his face all over the internet like it was going to bring him back. People who didn't even care about him when he was here. The routine was getting old to me.

#HANDSUPDONTSHOOT
#ICANTBREATHE
#SAYHERNAME

The list goes on.

It happened so often I was unsure why people protested in the first place; it didn't seem to change much. In my mind, the best way to go about life was to get money and stay out the way. That's what I saw my dad do. *Things are the way they are*, he'd say. Besides, it wasn't like any protest in the history of ever *needed* Cooper King.

But something about last weekend's shooting hit different this time. Not only was it my city, but Samir was one of us. This time it felt personal, because it was.

Even though we were about a mile from the strip, I could already hear the chaos churning. Sirens wailed as ambulances and cop cars sped toward H Street, a popular thoroughfare with bars and retail storefronts. It wasn't always that way, but with the city changing, H Street had become a go-to for transplants and hipster types. I still remember the H Street of before, one you didn't necessarily want to be caught on after 11 p.m. when the stores closed, and anyone still out there was pushing or using.

Ghetto birds flew overhead, capturing footage of an unruly DC, as residents and Black Lives Matter protesters took to the streets. You could even hear the faint chants and cries from the people marching.

"You got that?" Jason asked. He didn't look at anyone in particular, but I knew he was talking to Rico, his right-hand man.

Without responding, Rico reached in his waistband and pulled out a small, silver revolver with a shiny black handle. He handed it to Jason, who tucked it away in the back pocket of his already sagging shorts. Jason looked back and caught my gaze. I felt embarrassed, like I had just seen something I wasn't supposed to.

"For protection only," he said, staring straight at me.

I nodded in understanding and tried to keep pace with the long strides of him and his boys. Altogether it was four of us, dressed in black and green fatigues. Jason, Rico, me, and one other dude I didn't know.

Rico was one of Jason's homies from the sandbox, a day one. He was a tall, slim dude with tattoos covering his whole body. He had long locs that reached his shoulders and always kept a blunt in his hand. He reminded me of Wiz Khalifa.

He used to live on the block but I hadn't seen him in quite some time. Come to find out, he had got locked up and recently came home from DC jail. He was trying to turn things around and get back on his feet, according to Jason. But seeing him produce a firearm made me think he hadn't quite turned the corner just yet.

Even though I didn't know the other guy mobbing with us, I recognized him. We were all from the same neighborhood. I was definitely the youngest there, but they all respected me because of Jason.

TOCOTOCOTOCOTO . . .

Our necks craned up at the ghetto bird circling above us, headed toward the marching crowd on the strip.

"Mask up," Jason called out, throwing on his red Pooh Shiesty. Rico covered his face with a black bandanna and the mystery homie with us pulled down his red beanie, revealing a mask with a skull printed on the front. I followed suit, covering my face, as we made a right off Seventeenth Street and onto the edge of H Street where the protest had just begun.

My heart raced as we walked up on a sea of people that had taken over the entire strip. I wasn't sure what to expect because I had never been to an actual protest.

The air was electric with anticipation, a mix of determination and hope. The energy made my skin tingle with goosebumps. The protesters were a mosaic of different faces, people of all ages, colors, shapes, and sizes, moving as one. Some were holding hands, some throwing fists in the air. There were voices shouting as loud as they could, chanting messages filled with both passion and pain. It was powerful.

"NO JUSTICE, NO PEACE! NO JUSTICE, NO PEACE!" the crowd shouted in a unified call-and-response. It was like the group had rehearsed the march beforehand. Bold signs rose high above the crowd, each one with a profound phrase scribed on them.

**RESPECT BLACK LIVES
LIKE YOU RESPECT BLACK CULTURE**

SILENCE IS VIOLENCE

**RACISM IS A DISEASE.
REVOLUTION IS THE CURE**

The trolley that runs H Street was frozen on the tracks and some of the shops, coffee spots, and bars were already boarded up, prepared for any potential attacks. A couple stores even had signs in the windows that said things like POC OWNED or BIPOC OWNED as a sort of plea to not be destroyed. None said BLACK OWNED though, and I guess that was part of the problem.

As we passed through the crowd, I felt a sense of unity that was comforting. It felt like a pep rally at school before a big game and we were all on the same team ready to face off against a common enemy.

"This way," Jason called out, his voice muffled from the mask covering his face.

He took a hard right off the main street and we all followed, peeling away from the larger group before taking a quick left into the long alleyway behind the storefronts.

It grew eerily quieter as the freedom marching fell to a faint lull. Instantly I felt even more exposed being away from the large crowd. Jason picked up his pace, trying to get ahead of the protest.

My eyes darted around and noticed cameras at the back doors of a few of the stores. I didn't mind much because my face was covered, but nevertheless I tried to keep my head down and move quickly. Suddenly Jason slowed to a stop.

"This is it," he announced.

Rico checked our surroundings, likely looking for witnesses, cops. I looked around myself, searching for a reason to back out. The nervousness I felt in Jason's basement returned with a vengeance as my stomach twisted. My ski mask was soaked from my sweating beneath it and my heart was beating so hard I thought it'd fly out of my chest.

Jason put on a pair of black tactical gloves and his crew did the same. I certainly hadn't gotten the "bring gloves" memo. It felt like a bad omen, but at that point I was in too deep.

Jason walked up to the back of Moe-Town, a popping boutique in the city full of high-end street fashion and designer clothes. Off-White, Fear of God, rare Jordans, exclusive DC fashion, Moe-Town had anything you could want. I had to admit, it was the perfect target.

He checked the door; locked, of course.

"Rico, it's on you," he said, backing away.

Rico stepped up and pulled something I couldn't see out of his pocket.

"Get in place, Coop," Jason threw my way.

I watched the alleyway while trying to see what Rico was doing. It looked like he was fiddling with the lock until his head popped up—

"Got it," he announced. And like magic, the back door of the store sprang opened.

"Let's go!" Jay shouted, stepping through the doorway into the store, followed by Rico and then the mystery homie that was with us.

Me, I was frozen in place.

A quick flash of conscience came over me with fear beating down on my spirit. My dad always told me, "*Listen to your gut, Coop,*" and right now I was doing the best I could to ignore my very loud gut. Stealing was never okay, I knew this. And I definitely wasn't the type of kid that would do well in jail. *Jail?!*

Suddenly I was alone in the alley with a chance to run away and forget this whole thing ever happened.

The upside, I told myself, was that Jason said all I had to do was look out for any trouble and signal if I saw movement. Easy enough. I wouldn't even need to get my hands dirty. So I shook the feeling and planted my feet. I was committed.

It was tax season.

CHAPTER TWO
COOPER
CLOSE CALL

Jason and his friends moved through the store so quickly they looked like shadows bouncing around the room. I peered back down the alley, stretching my neck around the brick wall to make sure the coast was still clear.

I somehow thought being the lookout would be safer than doing the actual looting, and maybe it was. But it didn't feel that way. My eyes were the size of golf balls as my head turned side to side, ready to signal if I saw any police activity.

"Yo, Coop!"

"Yo?!" I called shakily, keeping my eyes on the alley.

"Grab that duffel," Jason called out.

I did a double take. *Whatyoumean?!* I didn't believe I'd heard him correctly, sure that the mask covering his face had contorted his words. I slowly followed his eyeline over to a chocolate brown leather duffel bag sitting on the shelf.

"Hurry!"

Turned out, I had heard him loud and clear. Jason was asking me to steal.

The soles of my shoes must've melted into the scorching

asphalt because my feet wouldn't budge. Of course, I didn't want to go. But caught up in the fever of the moment, it didn't feel like the right time to argue with Jason, or disobey him.

I gritted my teeth as I did what I was told and stepped through the doorway. On the way in, a jagged piece of metal near the bottom of the doorframe sliced my calf. It felt like fire shooting through my body. I swallowed my scream, thankful my mask was covering my twisted face.

I limped past the other boys ripping through the store, trying not to put too much pressure on my wound as a cool trickle of blood made its way down my leg. I hastily snatched up the duffel bag from Jason and headed back for the alley just as quickly.

"Coop, where you going? Fill it up!" Jason called out, frantically stuffing a bag of his own.

I thought cameramen would jump out from behind the mannequins and tell me this was some prank. Some funny bit to post on social media. But Jason was dead serious. I looked at him, pleading with my eyes, begging him to let me leave. But all he did was give a resounding nod, encouraging me to do what he was asking. It was like he was hazing me and I couldn't understand why.

I steeled myself, turned to the nearest clothing rack and quickly began filling up the bag. With every garment I snatched off the hanger, I felt like I was digging myself into a deeper and deeper grave. I kept stuffing the bag, praying it would fill up fast so I could leave. But apparently it was a magical, bottomless bag because it wouldn't run out of space.

CRASH!!

I nearly jumped out of my socks when a deafening boom echoed from the front of the store. When I turned to look, I saw the front window was busted out and light was shining in, but only for a second, because the next moment the gaping hole was filled with the bodies of other looters pouring inside.

Even though Jason's face was covered, I knew he was smiling from ear to ear under that mask. His plan had worked exactly like he said it would. *We just gotta be the first in, first out. Others will come to take the heat off us*, he'd told me.

As the other looters filed in, Jason, Rico and Skull Face bolted for the back door. I took off after them, as I finished throwing one last pair of jeans in the bag.

I stepped through the door, more carefully this time, and out into the alley.

"Split up?" Rico asked.

"For sure, meet y'all on the block," Jason agreed. "Stay low, and keep y'all's face covered!"

They quickly dapped and scattered. Jason and Skull Face took off down the alley and Rico sprinted up the street away from the protest.

I was stunned. The plan had always been for me to be the lookout while the crew hit the store. Afterward, we were all going to split up, and I was supposed to head to the protest to blend in for a while before leaving the scene. But I wasn't supposed to have stolen goods with me! I didn't know what else to do, so I stuck to at least part of the plan and adjusted the duffel bag on my shoulder as I headed down the block toward the chaos.

When I hit H Street it was even more of a mess than before.

We couldn't have been in the store for more than five minutes and already the scene outside had completely changed. The streets were now filled with clusters of bodies running in and out of different buildings on the strip, looting sneaker stores, a skate shop, and even a CVS.

It was almost like the attack was coordinated.

The far end of H Street had been blocked off by MPD squad cars and a militarized police force in riot gear, preventing anyone from reaching Union Station. They were slowly advancing, preparing to shoot gas and smoke into the stores that were being robbed and ransacked. The protesters were headed back toward Seventeenth Street, so I jogged gingerly in their direction, hoping to catch up and blend in.

My heart was pounding from adrenaline and I was almost hyperventilating. I wanted so badly to lift my ski mask, just long enough to catch my breath, but I thought against it. I couldn't be careless.

The street was littered with trash from knocked-over garbage cans, broken signs, and other debris. A small fire even burned in the middle of the street made of newspapers and an American flag.

TOCOTOCOTOCOTO...

The helicopter flew overhead again and I quickly looked down to keep hidden. I had never been in any serious trouble before, but for the first time, I felt like I'd done something that could land me in just that.

When the cop first killed Samir, Jason asked me how it made me feel. I was honest—I told him it made me angry. He asked me what I was planning to do about it, and I was honest again. Nothing.

The second I'd said it I felt ashamed.

"What can I do?" I quickly asked, looking for redemption.

"You can take what's yours. They put us through collective trauma, repeatedly. You know what that does to our mental, seeing Black people murdered all the time? They owe us."

He wasn't wrong.

It's the way old heads on the block would talk when they got drunk. Revolutionary and such as they moaned about the Black man's plight in America. It was their way of licking their wounds.

"Every time they take one of ours, it's tax season," Jason continued. "Time to hit the streets. I'm done with the peaceful marching. I'm robbing and looting from now on and I'll use that bread to build up the neighborhood, on some real Robin Hood type shit."

Despite it all sounding like not the best way to go about things, I recognized Jason had found something to believe in.

It was a conversation I shouldn't have even entertained, but for some reason I just kept listening. Maybe because I didn't have a summer job and with Mom gone, money was tight. Dad was working multiple shifts to keep the lights on and I saw this as an opportunity to help him with bills around the house. Or maybe I kept listening because Jason was the closest thing I had to a big brother and on some level, I wanted to please him. Maybe a combination of both.

Back when my mom had still been here, she must've asked him to look after me one time on a walk to the store, and Jason, being the passionate kid he was, kept that energy my whole life. In elementary, he would walk me and his little sister to school. And coming up, I was always the coolest kid in class just because of my affiliation with Jason. That was my big bro.

But as we got older, our paths went very different ways. At nineteen, Jason got expelled from high school and never quite bounced back. He started hanging with some of the other guys in the neighborhood and over time, my dad got uncomfortable with me moving around the city with him.

Bullets ain't got no name, he'd say. I couldn't argue with that.

Still, back in the day, when we were kids, I would spot for Jason all the time. We'd walk down to the liquor store and I'd distract the clerk while Jason grabbed us some Utz crab chips and a couple of AriZona iced teas.

I hadn't done anything like that since we were kids, but maybe that was part of the reason I'd agreed to loot with him. For old times' sake. Not to mention the convincing sincerity in his eyes when he'd asked me to join in.

I'd never said the truth to him about the plan—that I was scared. That wasn't something you were supposed to say on my block.

"Okay. I'm down," I'd said instead, only sounding half sure. Jason patted me on the back, and just like that, I was in.

At the time, I'd brushed it off, thinking there probably wouldn't be any protests to begin with. And if so, maybe Jason would get cold feet or replace me with one of his other homeboys, or any number of things to get me out of the commitment.

I was wrong.

"NO JUSTICE!" a distorted voice boomed over a megaphone at the front of the crowd, snapping me to my present reality.

"NO PEACE!" the crowd shouted back.

I had been so focused on getting back home I didn't realize I was standing in the middle of the protest. The people around me slowed to a stop, but I pushed through the crowd toward the front. Being surrounded by these faces made me feel less exposed. Some of the protesters had backpacks on and some wore masks, so I didn't stick out much now and that put me at ease.

When I reached the front of the crowd, I froze. I could even feel my jaw drop a little. The last person in the world I expected to see was standing a few feet in front of me, holding the megaphone.

It was *Monique*.

Monique was perfect in every way. We grew up together on the block and even my earliest memories of her consist of me being head over heels. The best way to describe her is she was *the one*. She was the smartest in every class, was the president of the National Honor Society, and had won all the science fairs in school. But she was also athletic and captain of both the basketball and track teams, and was proven to have hands after a couple run-ins with girls from rival schools. But she was also a poet and an activist and spoke beautifully at all the school functions. Talk about a girl who could do it all.

And to top it all off, shorty was just downright beautiful, with an infectious smile you couldn't help but be smitten by. Her jet-black hair contrasted so nicely against her smooth brown skin, the color of a perfectly baked chocolate chip cookie. But most importantly she was real. Real was hard to find, and I adored her for it.

Only problem was, she was Jason's little sister.

Monique's voice boomed over the megaphone as people cheered her on. "**The revolution will not be televised. The revolution will be streamed, through Windows, laptops, smartphones, and screens. The revolution will be posted, liked, and shared from your Microsoft devices and MacBook Airs. The revolution will be found by internet-scrolling teens, settled between those lighthearted memes . . .**"

I couldn't leave. I was glued, hanging on her every word. She was a natural leader, much like Jason. Though the way they approached things was completely different.

Monique was shouting her poem at the militarized police blocking the road. Men and women in dark uniforms and padded body armor. They were faceless, their identities hidden beneath cold, black balaclava masks and helmets. The only thing you could see were their piercing eyes.

With both ends of H Street blocked off, they had us trapped like mice in a maze. To get home I'd have to go around them.

"**It is very, very important that we keep this moment as peaceful as possible. As peaceful and as organized as possible. In memory of Samir. In memory of Davon Marcus, who was killed years ago in a similar fashion. In memory of all the Black and Brown men, women, and children killed by police. Because they want us to mess up. They want us to be disorganized and disreputable, but not today!**"

After the shock of seeing Monique wore off, I realized she

was talking about the looters. She was talking about us. She was talking about *me*.

I looked around to see how people were responding and, to my surprise, was met with the judgmental glare of a few protestors. I turned and saw I had more eyes watching me from the other side.

You're being paranoid, Cooper, I told myself. *It's no way they know you're with the looters.*

"Yo, you with those looters?" a voice called out. It was a big dude with a white bandanna wrapped around his face.

I looked down at my hands. *How stupid.* The tags were still dangling off the brand-new duffel bag I was carrying. A dead giveaway. I was caught red-handed.

"We not with that, homie. Take it somewhere else," the dude said before I could even respond to his question. I tried to ignore him, but could hear murmurs from the other demonstrators closing in around me.

"Brother, we hope you're not doing something unlawful in the name of our peaceful protest," Monique called out from the front of the crowd.

I locked eyes with Mo and this strange feeling came over me, like she could see through my mask. Like she could tell from the set of my shoulders and the guilt coursing through my body that it was me.

Slowly the protestors started to surround me, jeering and mouthing off. Suddenly the peaceful mob seemed like the most dangerous place for me to be.

My palms turned sweaty as I searched around for a hole in the crowd to make an exit. The police started to step forward to see what the commotion was about and the voice in my head started to panic, screaming for me to make a run for it.

A protestor grabbed for my duffel bag and we started to tug back and forth as the crowd grew rowdier and closed in tighter.

"Hold on! Hold on!" Monique shouted, but it was too late. The gloves were off. Metaphorically.

I tugged at the duffel bag, trying to pry it from the random man in the crowd.

"Stop! Stop!" Mo shouted.

When all of a sudden—

BANG . . . BANG!

We froze for a hair of a second because we all knew what that sound was.

Gunshots.

Everyone erupted into absolute pandemonium, screaming, ducking down, and running every which direction.

But me, I was planted. I looked for Monique.

She was nowhere in sight.

Where'd she go?! I tried to rush to the spot where she'd just been standing, but the crowd was like an ocean wave that carried me with it. I frantically scanned around, but none of the panicked faces were Mo's. Quick-moving bodies blocked my view.

The officers on the front line sprang into action, equipping themselves with high-tech masks and firing tear gas and smoke bombs that filled the air. They interlocked to form a solid wall with their shields, and started to march forward with a calculated precision like those warriors from the movie, *300*. It was intimidating.

As much as I was terrified for Mo and wanted to make sure she was good, I couldn't stay any longer. My throat was burning and my eyes started to water; pretty soon I wouldn't be able to see a thing. I shielded my eyes as I bolted for a side street to make my way around the barricade. The gas and smoke in the air made it hard to navigate through the maze of people. I could barely breathe as my heart pounded against my chest with a heavy *thump*. The deafening shouts and shattering of glass shrouded my ears, making me dizzy. It felt as if I was trying to escape some sort of war zone.

I dashed through a narrow alley, emerging onto a wider street. By now I was moving as fast as my feet could carry me. I glanced back to make sure I was alone as a lump formed in my throat, and suddenly—

THUD!

I ran into something solid and stumbled backward, landing hard on my backside. My duffel bag made a clanging metallic sound as it dropped somewhere out of my reach. I peered through the thick smoke, coughing and struggling to see. I could barely make out a figure moving through the smoke but it was large and blue.

My heart sank when I realized I had crashed right into a cop.

I felt around to get my bearings as I realized the cop was thrown off-balance too. He seemed to search for something of his own on the ground. I whipped my head left and right and through the fog, saw what he was looking for. It wasn't my bag that had made that clanging sound; it was his gun, just a few feet away from me.

Time seemed to slow almost to a standstill, and I could almost hear my own thoughts echoing in my head. *Stay down, Coop! Stay down.*

But I couldn't go to jail. Especially not for looting clothes I hadn't even wanted to take in the first place. Even still, staying down and not resisting seemed like the safest, most logical thing to do.

But there was something in the back of my mind gnawing at me.

It was Samir.

The chance that this officer would shoot me for absolutely nothing felt oddly . . . high. Visibility wasn't great and I had technically just assaulted him. Not to mention the recent gunshots. Samir was killed for way less.

Another option popped into my head. I could . . . grab the gun.

I had never held a gun before and now didn't seem like the time to start, even though it was probably my only hope at backing the officer down enough to get away.

"FREEZE!" the cop shouted in frustration, finally spotting the gun beside me.

For a second, I thought about putting my hands up and doing what he said.

But only for a second.

CHAPTER THREE
COOPER
BAD NEWS

"What are you passionate about, Cooper?" my pops had asked me just twenty-four hours earlier.

He'd seen me coming out of Jason's basement and I'm sure he could smell the weed smoke, though I didn't personally partake. Even without the scent, I was worried I'd caught a contact high and he would notice.

My pops had grown up in the streets. He was just a kid when OGs like Curtbone ran Langston Terrace. Those were his role models. And as he grew up, he chased after the same things they possessed: money, power, respect.

But at sixteen, the same age as me, he almost lost his life in a beef with a rival crew. After that close call, he started a different path and never looked back. A path that led him to my mom and the rest is history. When she was here, she would tell me stories about my dad being a man I never really knew. Getting into fights, heavy drinking . . . smoking "reefer," she'd call it.

You'd think he'd be cool about most things, but more than anything my dad wanted something different for me, so sometimes he was overly protective. And it only got worse after my mom passed.

"I don't know what I'm passionate about," I told him. I truly didn't. Other than football there wasn't too much I was into. And it's not like I was going to the league or anything; I was an average athlete, if that. I only played ball to land some cool points with the honnies. To be honest, when my mom died, I felt like I lost the ability to possess passion. It's what caused Mo and I to grow apart.

"Well, you better figure it out because kicking it over there with them knuckleheads ain't gonna do you no good. Trust me, I know. You gotta find a passion. Like me."

My dad held up his fists. "Now I do something positive with these." My dad worked down at Amtrak fixing trains even though he spoke like he was healing the world.

"Okay, Dad. I hear you but you're wrong about Jason," I responded, annoyed that he had called my big bro a knucklehead.

I was watching Jason try to turn his life around and people on the outside never saw that in him. In a way it was like some chicken-and-the-egg shit. Did Jason become a knucklehead? Or did his own people make him one before he even had a chance to become something more?

"We were actually talking about going to the protest tomorrow. For Samir," I said, giving him a stern look. I wasn't lying, but I wasn't telling the whole truth either. Really, I just needed to say something to make him eat his words.

"Hmph," he snorted, "you better not go down there with them boys. Mess around and find yourself in a world of trouble."

My dad's words shocked me. I thought he'd be proud of me for standing up for a cause. Plus, my plan had backfired. I hated disobeying my pops, so I often omitted the truth instead. But I'd broken my usual rule: If he didn't know what I was doing, he couldn't tell me not to do it.

"Why not, Dad? This is like . . . history. What trouble could we get in at a protest?"

"Cooper, you are a young Black man in America. You can always get into trouble. That's why the best thing you can do is avoid situations where trouble is likely to occur. A police standoff is one of them."

That was the first time it hit me that there could be danger down at the protest. If I hadn't regretted my decision up to that point, my dad talking some sense into me surely cleared things up. Still, I'd made a promise to Jason. A promise I regretted after colliding with the cop at the protest.

But it was too late to turn back, so I did the only thing I could do. I ran. I Forrest Gump ran. Usain Bolt ran. Florence Griffith Joyner ran! I ran so fast I thought I'd grow wings right there and take off in flight.

When I finally looked up, I realized I had completely left H Street and was back on Seventeenth. My lungs burned, my legs ached, and my chest felt like it was on the verge of exploding, but I couldn't stop moving.

I looked back to see if the cop was following me, but he wasn't. Nobody was. The street was empty and I was alone again, although I could see and hear the chaos swirling down on H Street. It looked like the whole city had gone up in smoke.

I slowed to a quick walk and briefly lifted my ski mask just enough to take in as much air as I could and stop myself from shaking. I looked down at the stupid duffel Jason made me grab and ripped off the tag that almost got me caught then stuffed it in my pocket.

The sun had started to set by the time I was halfway to the block and the sky was a soft orange from the mix of dust and fire in the air. Once my adrenaline settled down and I knew I was safe, my mind settled on one thing.

Monique.

Panicked, I remembered searching—and not finding—her face in the crowd when shots rang off and I winced.

I quickly pulled out my phone, almost dropping it because my hands were shaking, and texted her.

> yooo Mo, where you? I was walking from the store and heard shots, you not around the way r u?

I shook my head at the lameness of having to lie. But no way I could tell Mo I was the guy in the crowd with the stolen goods. I hated that I even had to think about lying at a time like this. But even more, I hated that I wasn't able to jump to her side in that moment. I wouldn't be able to forgive myself if something had happened to her. I started to feel a lot like a coward. Then I started to feel frustrated that this whole thing was because of Jason.

Bzzt, bzzt . . .

Speak of the devil. A text from Jason.

> let's meet tomorrow, it's too much heat

I shook my head as I quickened my pace to get back home. I needed more than anything to look Jason in the eyes and find out why he'd betrayed my trust. Like, why would he ask me to steal when I specifically told him I was uncomfortable with it? It almost felt . . . deliberate. Something didn't add up.

When I hit my block, water bugs danced along the curb trying to avoid the streetlights. The soft hum of cicadas started to replace the sharp symphony of sirens. And a few fireflies flickered out in the distance. My favorite thing about DC was easily the summer nights. They usually calmed me, but right now, all I could think of was Mo.

My dad still wasn't home when I got in, which was a good thing because there was no chance he wouldn't have asked me about the huge duffel slung across my body.

Upstairs in my room I dropped the bag on the floor with the quickness. I hadn't realized how tired and bruised my shoulders and neck were. I looked down to the dried blood on my calf; the brim of my white sock had turned a reddish brown. My Nikes were scuffed and stained.

Monique's face popped into my head again. I didn't think she recognized me in the crowd, but the small chance she did worried me. I took out my phone again and called her but it went straight to voicemail. "*AGHHHH*," I growled to myself. Everything was a mess.

I fell back on the bed and took in the peace and quiet, telling myself that everything was going to be okay. Slowly my eyes drifted over to the duffel bag and some of my angst was suddenly replaced with curiosity.

Everything had gone from zero to a hundred so quick, I didn't even know what was in the bag I risked my life for.

I hoisted the duffel onto the bed, unzipped it and turned it upside down. High-end jeans, shirts, hoodies, and more came tumbling out. I checked the price tag of one of the jackets on the bed and couldn't believe what I was reading.

"*Oh shit* . . . ," I muttered to myself.

$1,199.99

My eyes almost popped out of my head, straining to make sure I was reading correctly. I checked another price tag.

$699.99

And another . . .

$395.99

As mad as I was at the whole scenario, I couldn't help but smirk just a little. I checked more and more price tags. The cheapest thing in the bag was two hundred dollars. Hell, even the bag itself was priced at $599.

Even though I wanted to punch Jason, maybe he was onto something. If every item I had was trending like this, my take was worth about six grand, and I planned to keep every bit of it for my trouble.

A thud coming from downstairs broke my concentration. Dad was home.

I hurried to stuff the stolen clothes back into the duffel bag and slid it under my bed. I threw on a pair of dirty sweats to cover my leg and quickly rinsed my face and hands to wash the madness off me.

"Cooper!" my pops called from downstairs.

"Hey, Dad," I called back, already heading to the stairs to greet him. When I finally laid eyes on him, he was already popping open a beer and plopping on the couch. I could tell how tired he was by how slowly he moved.

Since my mom passed, my pops had been putting in extra-long hours. Double shifts. He said it was because college was coming up and we needed to be prepared financially, but it felt a lot like he was drowning himself in work to escape the pain of losing the love of his life. Maybe it was a combination of both. In any case, money troubles were another reason he was on me about getting a job. I appreciated him for that, though it felt like an unnecessary stress he was taking on and then projecting onto me. Besides, I still wasn't sure college was the thing for me. I guess because I didn't really know what my *thing* was.

"How was work?" I asked, trying to make my voice sound as calm as possible. Mo still hadn't texted me back. I'd decided if I didn't hear from her in the next hour I'd need to walk across the street to her house.

"Work was work," he said with a sigh. "Traffic, now that was something else. Took me an extra hour to get home."

"Rush hour?"

"Nah, that riot! You didn't go down there, did you?"

I tried not to fidget. As a kid my dad was an expert at spotting when I was lying. But in the last few years I'd sharpened my poker face.

"Nah, you said not to," I said, heading down the stairs. "I was too busy filling out job applications."

He didn't respond immediately. I fought back the uneasiness creeping into my bones and played it cool.

"Good, because those knuckleheads destroyed everything," he said finally. I exhaled. "I don't know who raising these kids. In fact, I do—it's kids raising kids."

The judgmental tone in his voice was like nails on a chalkboard. Those were my friends he was talking about, but I didn't have the strength to engage.

"Did you take the chicken out to thaw like I texted you?" he asked, flipping on the TV.

"I forgot," I lied.

"Come on, Coop. Put it in some cold water, would ya? Please?"

"Yeah, my bad," I said. I stepped into the kitchen to take out the meat. He didn't seem to suspect anything and I imagined the cop I collided with would've pulled up by now if he had somehow followed me home, so I started to breathe a little easier.

When—

"Cooper!" he yelled from the other room. "Come here, look. This is what I was talking about!"

I walked into the living room and saw a reporter on TV, standing at a familiar scene—the rubble of the protest filled in the screen behind her as she spoke into the camera.

"*We come to you live from the H Street corridor, where a protest began this evening in response to the murder of Samir Edwards, a fourteen-year-old boy who was being apprehended for an alleged robbery . . ."*

"Oh, come on! Why they have to say it like that!?", my dad yelled at the TV. "It was a damn pickpocket, not no robbery."

He was right, but I couldn't respond; I was too focused on trying to hear what the lady on the screen had to say next. I felt like she might look right at my dad and say, "And Cooper King was down here when he knows his ass shouldn't've been."

But she said something far worse.

"The protest started as a peaceful demonstration but tragically turned deadly . . ."

I stopped in my tracks. Deadly?

I thought about the gunshots that rang off and wondered if the two could be connected somehow. They had to be. My next thought was Monique. *Oh shit.* I held my breath waiting for more info. She still hadn't hit me back and my mind began to entertain intrusive thoughts. *Could something really have happened to her?* I started to think of all the moments she flashed that beautiful smile at me, lifting my spirits anytime I felt down. I tried not to panic too much.

The segment featured clips of the protest. First, people chanting in the street, peacefully marching in solidarity. Then, shaky social media and camera phone images of masked teens running in and out of stores, taking whatever they could get their hands on.

Then, in a dark turn, the footage showed yellow tape that marked off an entire street crowded with cops. The street looked familiar. It was just off the alley we walked through to get to the store we looted.

"Just one block away from where the protest started, a young woman was murdered. Her identity has not been released."

"*Oh jeez, no,*" I muttered to myself, rubbing my eyes.

"I know, right?" my dad said, putting his hand to his forehead. "I can't believe those kids did that. God help us."

But I couldn't engage with my dad, not at that moment. Too many thoughts raced through my head. Jason and his gun, the gunshots at the protest, his text saying there was too much heat. *What did he mean by that?*

Did he know about the murder somehow? I thought about Monique again, could something have happened to her?! I was on the verge of completely freaking out!

"Police would like to question these suspects and are seeking any information from community members and protest attendees."

My eyes and ears locked in as the talking head cut to helicopter footage showing the suspected triggermen.

"Good! I hope they catch them too!" my dad continued to shout at the TV with a scowl on his face.

But I couldn't say a thing. I was in shock. The news anchor's voice seemed distant, muffled by the sudden rush of adrenaline that ran through my veins. My body flushed with heat as disbelief washed over me. I couldn't believe what I was seeing—it was *us* on the screen. Jason, Rico, Skull Face, and me, walking through a back alley in shorts and cutoff tees, our faces covered by masks. Panic and confusion spun in my mind.

What *had* Jason done? How were *we* being labeled as suspects in a murder?

The screen cut to a large police officer walking up to a podium.

He didn't look like a typical cop. He wore a white dress shirt with a sharp, black tie. He had four gold stars on each shoulder and a medal pinned over his heart. He looked like he meant business as he adjusted his mic.

"*We are saddened by this tragedy that has occurred on the heels of so many others. We do have great reason to believe that one of the men seen in the footage is the gunman. He and his coconspirators will be caught swiftly and brought to justice just as fast. To the fullest extent of the law.*"

Gunman? Coconspirators? The room was spinning and suddenly I felt like I was in a dream. There must've been some mistake. There was no reason we should be suspects in a murder. No reason *I* should be a suspect at least.

"Cooper?" my dad called out, briefly silencing the alarms going off in my head. "You okay?"

He stared at my shocked face and I knew I must look like I saw a ghost.

"Yeah, I'm good."

But I was far from good. I needed to find Monique. And I needed talk to Jason ASAP and find out what in the hell was going on.

CHAPTER FOUR

COOPER
WHERE'S JASON?!

Light shone through my bedroom window as the sun rose, but I was already wide awake. Instead of sleeping, I'd tossed and turned through the night, hoping that Mo was able to escape H Street alive and well. Hoping that everything I saw on the news was a waking nightmare.

I, Cooper King, was a murder suspect?!

It's not like I could go tell the cops all I knew. I didn't know anything. And I wasn't even identified so there was no reason to go tell on myself. But the longer I didn't say anything, the guiltier I seemed. What if I left fingerprints in that store? What if I left behind a drop of blood from the cut on my leg? I wasn't prepared for any of this. I needed to talk to Jason and I needed to know Monique was okay.

I checked my phone and the text I had sent to Jason the night before.

> yo, u seen the news??

But he still hadn't responded.

I checked the text I had sent to Mo but she hadn't responded either. I needed to get up, but I could barely move, frozen by the idea that something had happened to Mo, and somehow, I may be held responsible.

A small part of me started to resent Jason. Sure, over the years we'd grown apart but the love and respect I had for him never wavered. But I was starting to feel like that love had blown up in my face. It was like he didn't value me the same way I valued him, and that's what hurt the most. Maybe my dad was right about him.

I clicked over to check my socials to see if any new news broke. BIG mistake.

My entire feed was filled with videos and pictures of the protest. The name of the person that was tragically killed still hadn't been released but people were already posting their RIPs and condolences, calling for the mayor to find the kids that committed the crime and serve them justice.

A knot the size of a basketball started to churn in my stomach. *It'll be okay, Coop. You can't get in trouble for something you didn't do . . . right?*

But then I thought about what my dad said. A Black kid like me could get in trouble for anything.

Best-case scenario was they find the shooter. Fast.

Justice would be served. Police wouldn't need to find the phantom kids running the streets and I could go on about my life. My dad would never know I disobeyed him. Monique would never learn about my involvement in the looting. I'd still make a few grand this summer and life would go on.

But then there was the worst-case scenario. The scenario where the police never find the shooter but uncover our identities. That terrified me. If we ended up in that scenario, I could easily see the cops pinning this whole thing on us.

And my alibi was paper thin.

I'd been right there in the heart of the protest when the shots rang out. If clearing my name meant having to admit to looting, I'd do it, however much I dreaded it.

Still, that wasn't solid. Nobody could ID me at the store if it came to it.

My chest burned at the thought of getting in even the slightest trouble with the law. It's the one thing my mother begged of me as a kid, to stay out of trouble. *Once they get you, they've got you*, she'd say. I wouldn't be able to stand the look on my dad's face, seeing me handcuffed and lowered into a police car, or sporting a too-big suit and tie with my head hung low, standing in front of a judge and jury. He'd feel like he failed my mom. Shoot, I would too.

How could I be sure they'd never learn it was us in those ski masks? I couldn't find a good answer. And I was kicking myself for being in this position in the first place, but it was just another thing I couldn't control. I couldn't change the past.

I figured unless somebody snitched, the laws would not be able to tie the grainy news footage to us. Honestly, I was still unsure why we were suspects in the first place. But something told me Jason or the other boys might be able to shed some light on that. *That's it*, I thought. Maybe I find one of the other boys.

Bzzt, bzzt . . .

I jumped to my phone, hoping Jason had finally texted me back, but it wasn't him—it was Monique.

> Mo: Hey Coop, you up?

I let out the biggest exhale of my life. If there were two ten-ton stones pressing down on my shoulders, one of them just lifted. I was over the moon that Mo was at least breathing.

But if she wasn't the murder victim, who was?

I froze for a second, unsure of how to respond. For as happy as I was that she texted me, I still didn't know if she knew I'd been down at the protest with Jason. And I would do *anything* to make sure she didn't find out.

> Coop: yooo, yea I am. what's good? I hit you up yesterday.

> Mo: yea I know, saw your text, free to walk me to h street? the mayor's speaking and I don't wanna walk alone. Plus it'd be good to see u 😊

Even with everything going on, she still managed to make me smile.

> Coop: of course, I got you

> Mo: k, meet you outside in 10!

I reeled backward and took a deep breath. The good news was Monique was alive and well and didn't seem to have any idea of my involvement in the looting, but the last thing I wanted to do was return to the scene of the crime. However, maybe this was a chance to get to Jason.

I quickly swung my legs out of the bed and threw on basketball shorts, a fresh white tee, and my New Balance 993s. After getting cleaned up, I gave myself a few dabs of cologne for good measure. It wasn't the time to be rizzing Mo up, but I hadn't spent much time with Mo since my mom died a year ago. I glanced down at the bracelet I never took off. My mom had given me the silver Cuban link bracelet when I turned ten and I hadn't taken it off since. In a way, it made me feel like she was still here with me.

Outside the air was thick like I knew DC summers to be. I looked up and down the street and spotted Jason's car, a burgundy '96 Chevy Impala, still parked exactly where it'd been yesterday. I couldn't understand why he was avoiding me. Maybe he felt bad for asking me to loot, or maybe he had seen the news too and was just as spooked as me. Whatever the reason, I was about to find out.

Being outside made me feel vulnerable, knowing the cops were looking for me. I still couldn't believe what was happening, but I needed to stay calm and think straight. And also so Mo wouldn't suspect anything out of the ordinary.

I practically sprinted across the street, took a deep breath, and knocked on Monique's door. After a moment she answered with her hair pulled back in a ponytail, wearing only a tank top and cheerleader shorts. I did my best to keep my eyes from dancing around her womanly figure.

"Cooooppppperrr," she said, jumping into my arms.

I held her close and for a brief second everything else slipped away. All my fears, anxieties, and worries were replaced by the sweet smell of her perfume.

"Yooo," I said, trying to play it cool even though things were definitely NOT cool. "How you feeling?"

"Ugh. I'm feeling all sorts of things. But come in, I was just finishing up, I'll be right back."

I stepped inside her small, dim living room and took a seat. Her house was just like mine but with way more decorations. Monique and Jason's mom was older than mine and her house reflected it. Family portraits covered almost every inch of the old wallpaper her mom had hung when she first bought the place, while trinkets and other knickknacks blanketed the end tables on each side of their couch.

"Yo, is Jason home?" I called to her as she headed upstairs.

"I don't think so, but you can check downstairs," she called back mid-stride.

As soon as she disappeared upstairs, I dropped the calm and collected act and hurried to the basement door that stood just at the mouth of the kitchen.

"Yo, Jay," I called out in a hushed voice, my face almost pressed against the wood frame. Nothing.

I knocked. Still nothing.

I turned the knob, gave a slight push, and the heavy door swung open into the darkness.

"Jay!" I called again, my voice echoing in the eerie silence.

I flipped the light switch on and made my way down the creaky steps. Jason definitely wasn't home, but I knew he'd been there by the slight differences I noticed from when I'd been there the day before.

The sheets on the bed were tossed instead of made and an

empty plate of food sat on a TV tray in front of the couch. But perhaps the biggest giveaway was the duffel bag full of stolen clothes protruding from the half-opened closet. I shook my head at his carelessness, walked over, and nudged the bag in deeper with my foot, then slid the closet door closed.

But there was one more thing that caught my eye.

A red, black, and green pamphlet on the coffee table. THE TIME IS NOW was written in huge letters across the front. I picked the pamphlet up and examined the front cover closely. Underneath the letters was the striking image of some creature with the head of a black wolf and the body of a lion, with green dragon-like wings spread wide.

"Coop?!" Monique called from upstairs.

I almost dropped the document on the table. For some reason I was feeling especially jumpy. Probably the guilt I felt.

"Coming!" I called while snapping a photo of the pamphlet. I ran back upstairs and found Monique dressed and ready to go.

"You good?" she asked, a hint of suspicion in her voice.

"Yep," I said, wiping my brow. "I borrowed a game and just wanted to return it," I lied. Monique nodded and that was that.

"Well come on, I don't want to be too late," Mo said, leading me out the front door.

As the lock clicked softly behind us, I tried to just settle into the warm feeling of being next to Mo. The whole city could've crumbled to dust around us, and I wouldn't have noticed. All I could think about was the relief that she was okay and the incredible guilt I felt for looting at a protest she clearly felt strongly about.

"So, uhhh, what's this about the mayor?" I asked, breaking the ice as we stepped off her porch.

"She's addressing the city about what happened yesterday. And I want to see if she's going to take accountability or spin the story," Mo answered pointedly.

"Accountability for what?" I asked, genuinely curious.

"For the way they've completed abandoned the city's youth. It's why things are the way they are. But I have a feeling they're going to blame this whole thing on our peaceful protest. You heard about what happened, right? The murder at the protest?"

I bit my bottom lip. Part of me just wanted to come out and tell Mo the truth about everything, but my guilt wouldn't let me.

On the other hand, Mo was good at solving problems. I remembered one time when I'd dropped my headphones in a subway vent on the sidewalk. I was ready to give it up when Mo bought a pack of gum, found the longest, slimmest branch she could, and made a contraption to fish out my headphones. That was Mo. Maybe she could help me with this problem, too.

"Yeah, I uh, heard things got pretty crazy," I said, scratching my head.

She looked up at me, her face full of emotion My heart skipped as I imagined her saying, *You liar, I know you were there!* But instead she just said, "Crazy doesn't even begin to describe it, Coop. This was the first protest I helped organize and we were ambushed."

Damn. As if I hadn't already felt bad, seeing Mo so torn up just made me feel lower than low.

"Ambushed?" I asked, my heart racing.

"Yeah," Mo replied, her nostrils flaring. "I mean, the looters must've intentionally chosen to use our movement to further their own agenda, like those anarchists a while back. We weren't down there for even an hour before the street was swarming with people only there to cause destruction!" she finished, throwing her hands in the air.

Monique's words hit me too hard. If there was ever any chance of me confiding in her about what was going on, it just flew out the window. She was pissed! And I couldn't have her pointing that anger at me.

"And now all people are talking about are riots and not the cause. Not Samir."

"Yeah, it's messed up," I muttered, my voice barely audible.

Her gaze narrowed, as if searching for a hidden truth. "Why couldn't Jason be more like you, Coop? You've always been your own person." Monique's eyes locked onto mine, filling me with even more guilt.

I swallowed hard. "Yeah, I guess. I mean I heard about it, but my pops ain't want me down there." Another half-truth to soothe my worries.

A heavy sigh escaped Monique's lips. "And then the shooting. I was there, Coop. I heard the shots. Someone lost their life, protesting the loss of a life. When does it end?" Mo cried out.

My mind spun, torn between the desire to connect with her and the fear of judgment and rejection. The more she spoke, the more real my situation felt and anxiety crept in. I had nothing to say, nothing to offer, because I was dead wrong. So I just kept asking questions.

"What do you think we can do to change it?" I asked. It was a question I never thought about until that moment, and after I said the words, I kind of hoped she had an answer.

Monique's brows furrowed, her face covered in uncertainty. "I don't know, Coop. It's overwhelming. But we have to start somewhere. Which is why I need to go see the mayor."

Her words resonated with me, stirring a fire. I tried to stay focused but her passion was intoxicating. Everything in me wanted to take her hand in mine and tell her everything would be okay, but that level of intimacy would be nothing short of weird.

Monique and I had a complicated relationship. As kids, we'd been inseparable. We spent endless hours exploring the alleyways behind our houses where we weren't supposed to be, or down at the rec center running amok on the playground. We were partners in crime, sharing our secrets and dreams. Our hopes and fears. But there was one moment, one single moment that changed everything.

It happened a couple years ago. Me, her, and a group of friends were all playing hide-and-seek after dark at the park not too far from our house. I was It, and I knew exactly where to find Monique. We shared all the same hiding spots. I checked the tunnel behind the pool and sure enough found Monique hiding there, but she didn't run. It was almost like she was waiting for me.

We stood there in the dim light and our eyes locked. The space between us seemed to evaporate as we closed in on each other. I leaned in and she leaned in. And . . . I kissed her. It was a brief, innocent peck, but I'll never forget the shock waves that went through my body.

After that day, things became complicated. We never talked about the kiss and instead pretended it never happened. Coming up, we were always like brother and sister, so looking back, I think we thought it was wrong. But maybe it wasn't. Maybe it was right. I'd never say that to her though because, honestly, I was intimidated.

A few months after that kiss my mom passed and I pretty much stopped engaging at all. I think Mo reminded me of my mom in some ways and being around her brought up too many feels.

But being by her now only felt right.

When we finally made it down to H Street, the air crackled with an unsettling energy. The aftermath of the protest and riot was palpable, as the bustling strip crawled with onlookers snapping pictures and sightseeing. Some buildings bore the scars of fire, the blackened remains serving as a haunting reminder and a stark contrast to the vibrant storefronts that once lined these streets.

Shop owners emerged from their stores, brooms in hand, attempting to sweep away the debris and remnants of the rioters. I watched as their weary faces mirrored the state of their businesses—some crying, their tears mixing with the ashes and dust that clung to their cheeks. Their dreams and hard work had been reduced to rubble. It was a heartbreaking sight.

I couldn't help but feel a sense of guilt. The reality of my secret participation in the looting gnawed at my conscience even more now. Not only had I contributed to this destruction, but I was at risk of facing heavy consequences for it.

"There she is," Monique said, breaking through my thoughts.

Up ahead Mayor Jackson stood on a small platform surrounded by armed security, addressing a sea of concerned residents and journalists. Monique and I walked up to the back of the tense crowd. *Click-click-click-click.* Cameras snapped as she prepared to speak.

"We are deeply saddened by the events that unfolded during the protest," Mayor Jackson said somberly, her voice amplified through the microphone on the podium. "We are committed to ensuring the safety of our citizens and bringing those responsible for this senseless violence to justice."

A hush fell over the crowd as a journalist raised a hand. "Mayor Jackson, can you provide any updates on the ongoing murder investigation? Is there any progress in catching the gunmen responsible for the crime?"

The mayor took a moment, her expression unsure, before responding. "Yes, we have made significant progress in the murder investigation, and just minutes ago made public that we've arrested one of the suspects involved in the shooting. This suspect we believe was the triggerman. Our law enforcement officers are working tirelessly to apprehend the others involved."

I felt my shoulders relax for the first time in the last twenty-four hours. I hadn't heard anything from police, and Mo hadn't mentioned them either. That told me whoever the cops apprehended had to be unrelated to me, Jason, and the crew.

"Cooper," Monique whispered.

"Yeah?"

"Cooper, look."

I looked down at Mo's phone, searching for what she was calling my attention to.

And then I saw the mugshot.

The hairs on the back my neck stood at attention. I couldn't believe it.

"Cooper!" Monique called again, her face turning to horror.

"I see it" was all I could manage.

Jason was the triggerman suspect.

Suddenly I was faced with a worse scenario than I imagined before, a scenario I hadn't considered. A scenario where Jason *was* the triggerman. Monique turned to me, her eyes pleading for help. "Cooper, I need to get home! There's no way Jason *killed* anyone," she said in disbelief, holding back tears.

The Jason I knew wasn't a murderer, but the cops had their guy whether Jason was guilty or not. There was only one way to free him.

Only one way to free myself.

I needed to find the shooter.

though
PART TWO
CONFUSION

CHAPTER FIVE
MONIQUE
THE VISIT

UNTITLED

In the canvas of life, a sister's love paints in the brightest hue,
Always in hopes of painting a picture as bright as you.
My brother . . .
Protected me like no other, comforted me, consoled me,
The wing I stood under.
Rain, sleet, snow, hail, not even a meteor shower,
Can come between a love like ours.
In every whispered secret, in every playful fight,
A sister's love will forever shine its light.
From childhood games under a setting sun,
A bond unyielding, that's never undone.
To late-night talks and rides through the streets,
The lessons you've taught me I always will keep.
I am your sister, your friend, your ride or die,
I love you, my brother, keep your head held high.

I folded my poem and put it back in my pocket. I planned to give it to my brother when we saw him down at the jailhouse. Rain pelted the windshield as I stared out at the blurry world beyond. The city was such a mess, much like my life at that moment. My head was still spinning from the news of Jason being arrested, so much so I thought it'd twist right off my shoulders.

I glanced over at my mom, Sarah, in the driver's seat. She looked pale, her knuckles white as they gripped the steering wheel. We didn't say much; there were no words that could make this nightmare disappear.

Besides, I already knew what she was thinking, that this was all her fault in some way or that she had failed Jason. But that couldn't be further from the truth.

Growing up there were two things my mother preached to me and Jason relentlessly. Two things we *should not, could not* do in any circumstance.

Rule #1: No kids.

Rule #2: No jail.

That was her bible.

I knew Jason being arrested, and for murder of all things, was eating away at her. I didn't have the privilege of only worrying about Jason; I had to worry about my mother, too, and that made this whole thing all the more heavy.

"It's going to be okay, Mom," I said, feeling the tension in the car.

"I know it will, baby. This has to be a mistake. Jason? Murder? That's ridiculous."

I knew she meant it but still her voice was unsure. When

police officers sink their talons into the flesh of young Black men, they hold on tight, refusing to let go. What we knew to be ridiculous didn't matter to them. It was all about what story they could sell. As we sped through the rain-soaked streets of the city, I couldn't help but notice how the city had been torn apart. And our family had been torn apart with it.

Jason and I had always been close. Even though he was just three years older, he'd taken on the role of a father figure when our own dad had abandoned us. He'd taught me how to ride a bike, helped me with my homework, and had this incredible knack for making me laugh even when things were tough. He was the one who calmed me during thunderstorms and checked my closet for monsters. He was everything a big brother should be, and everything a dad should have been.

But I noticed a shift when he graduated from high school. He didn't get into any big schools. He attended community college for a bit, but it didn't suit him. Pretty soon it only became about making money, helping Mom. Which is why I think she's hard on herself about Jason's transition to small-time hustler.

We both knew he was doing something. Selling weed, boosting clothes. Anything but committing violent acts.

Could he have really changed right before our eyes, but I had been blind to it?

No, I couldn't believe it. I couldn't believe Jason was capable of taking another life, no matter how far he'd fallen.

Finally, we pulled up to the police station and parked out in the lot. My mom took a second to prepare herself for what she was walking into.

"You ready?" she asked. Even though she was looking at me, it felt a lot like she was asking herself.

"Yes, Momma."

"Okay, let's go."

We ran inside, covering our heads from the rain that still fell, relentless, as if it were mourning with us. My mom pulled open the heavy door and I stepped inside a foreign world where I didn't belong.

The fluorescent lights overhead cast harsh shadows on the blank white walls. It was nothing like I'd seen on TV or in movies. No dramatic music, no detectives in sharp suits. Just a sterile, eerie silence.

The two officers who sat at the front desk didn't bother to acknowledge us as we approached them.

"Hi, I'm here for Jason Simms," my mom said quietly, shame in her voice. One of the officers looked up with disgust.

"Have a seat, The detectives will be out momentarily."

Their response was just as cold as the linoleum floors below our feet, but we sat down on the hard bench and waited as we were told. Being in this place made me think of Jason in handcuffs, his face twisted with worry. He was all alone behind these walls. My heart ached for him, for us. I kept a strong face for Mom, but inside, I was crumbling.

After what seemed like forever two detectives called to my mother. "Ms. Simms?"

"Yes?" she said, standing.

"I'm Detective Martin, and this is my partner, Detective Hunter. Right this way, please."

My mom and I followed the detectives down a narrow hallway to a steel door with a small window in it. It reminded me of the doors at school.

We stepped inside the small interrogation room and the harsh lights stung my eyes. We sat in two small chairs across from the two detectives. Detective Martin, a middle-aged man with tired eyes, and Detective Hunter, a younger woman with a stern expression, exchanged glances before beginning to speak.

"Your son, Jason," Detective Martin began, his voice grave, "was arrested this morning in Northeast and we have reason to believe he may have been involved with a shooting that resulted in the death of twenty-six-year-old Melissa Davis."

"Jason didn't shoot anyone!" I snapped.

"Mo," my mom whispered, putting a hand on mine. "But my daughter is right. My son isn't that type of kid. He's one of the good ones." My mom's breath hitched, and her grip on my hand tightened. She leaned forward, her voice trembling.

Detective Hunter looked at Martin and sighed, leaning back in her chair. "Unfortunately, he's already confessed to being in the area during the murder."

The officers slid large printed photos across the table. They were similar to the pictures that had been shown on TV, but more detailed. The high angle clearly came from a store camera that caught Jason and his friends running through the back alleys off H Street, not far from where the murder took place. One of the large bodies was circled with a thick red marker.

"That one there is Jason. Again, he's already admitted to it."

"I've seen the news. All those kids were down there protesting.

I don't know how you get from that to murder," my mom shot back quick.

I sat back, proud of how she was handling the detectives.

The cops exchanged glances again before speaking. I was beginning to understand that meant bad news was coming.

"When we arrested him, he had a firearm on him. And though there were no casings found at the scene, the weapon he had matches the profile of the pistol that was likely used in this shooting. It doesn't look good for him."

My mom's face turned to stone. She didn't have a response to that. It was almost like she went into shock.

I felt bad because I knew about parts of Jason my mother didn't. Parts he couldn't show her to keep her safe. Still, carrying a gun didn't sound like the Jason I knew, let alone using it.

"So what, he was carrying a weapon!" I blurted. "Have you seen the crime levels in this city? Gun violence is at an all-time high and people need to protect themselves cause y'all sure ain't looking after us!"

"Monique!" my mom shouted, looking serious. "That's enough."

"This isn't fair. Why'd they search Jason anyway? Stop and frisk? Profiling? None of this is fair."

Detective Martin shifted in his seat, looking uneasy. "The reason we apprehended Jason was because we received an anonymous tip," he explained to my mom, avoiding my gaze. "So, as we've said, none of this looks good for your boy."

"My son," my mother corrected him.

"We believe Ms. Davis confronted Jason about the stolen

property, and in return he attacked her," Detective Hunter added.

My heart sank further. The detectives' words were like shadows closing in around us, and I could feel the weight of the unknown crushing my chest. I needed to know more, for Jason's sake.

What was this about an anonymous tip?

"What can we do?" my mom asked, sounding like she had already lost hope in Jason.

"Well, he's been appointed a lawyer, so you can decide if you want to stay with them or go in a different direction. But more importantly, if we can get Jason to cooperate, it can significantly help him in this case."

"Cooperate how?" my mom asked.

"As you can see there are three other men in this photo. If he can identify them, that would go a long way."

A glimmer of hope flashed across my mother's face, but it was useless. Jason took pride in his loyalty—there was no way he'd turn on his friends. Besides, where we're from, being labeled a snitch would only make Jason's life all the more difficult. Maybe even ours, too.

"Well, can we see him?" my mom asked.

"Not right now; we're still processing him. But we'll call as soon as he's ready."

I hated that they talked about him like a piece of property.

"And we'll set you up with his lawyer as well," they continued. "One last thing, do either of you know this woman?"

The cops slid a photo across the table of a brown-skinned woman with braids. She didn't look familiar to me.

Mom and I shook our heads.

"This is Melissa Davis. The victim. We're just trying to see if there is any other possible motive here, other than the leading theory of a robbery."

"I don't know this woman, and my son didn't do this. You'll be hearing from our attorney. Let's go, Mo."

At once my mom stood and started for the door. I gave the detectives a cold glare and took off after her.

When we got back to the car, she didn't say a word, but I knew what she was thinking. We had a fight ahead of us. We were the only people in Jason's corner and we needed to be warriors for him the way he would for us.

I buckled my seat belt as my mom took off. The rain had let up and the sun decided to come back out. And suddenly off in the distance I noticed a rainbow had come out. Even though we didn't see Jason as planned, I took it as a sign that things would work out.

Rainbows always reminded me of Cooper King. As kids we used to chase them after storms or find them in puddles at the park. If Jason was like the father I never had, Cooper King was like my other half, although our relationship was a bit more . . . complicated. We had grown up together and maybe even could've been a *thing*, as my mom would say, if fate had been kinder to us.

Since I was a little girl, I had the biggest crush on Cooper. He wasn't like the other boys. He was sweet and goofy and caring and funny. It didn't hurt that he was easy on the eyes. He was tall and slim, and naturally athletic. He had swag but wasn't a pretty boy. He had charm but wasn't a player type. And he was from the block but wasn't a thug. He was perfect.

But about a year ago his mom died and something changed. I tried to reach out, tried to be there for him, but he made it clear he didn't need or want anybody holding his hand through his loss. I didn't take it personally, but after a while I did fall back.

But now, with Jason gone and seeing that rainbow, I felt like I wanted to be comforted by him. I felt like I needed a hug from someone other than my mom. Someone I could shift some of this weight to. When Jason wasn't there, Cooper had always been that person for me.

Plus, with any luck, maybe he knew more about the guys running with Jason the day of the protest.

CHAPTER SIX

COOPER
BABY SLEUTHS

I tried not to panic as I stared down at the clothes at the foot of my bed.

Shit.

Staring back at me was thousands of dollars' worth of stolen goods potentially tied to a murder investigation. I needed to get rid of them ASAP.

I couldn't risk taking the duffel bag out of the house while my dad was home, but the minute he was gone, I'd planned to toss everything in a trash bag and dump it in a bin out back. I hated that 'cause I really did need the money, but offloading the goods was too risky.

The other thing weighing on me was Monique. With Jason arrested for a dang murder, things were getting pretty serious and the guilt of lying to her about me being with him was eating away at me. I needed to figure out what happened with Jason, and Mo was the perfect partner. She was the only person who would understand we couldn't go to the cops. But how could I do that and keep secret the fact that I was with Jason moments before the shooting? It felt like an impossible task.

I started to pull clothes out the duffel bag and stuff them into a trash bag when there was a knock at the door.

"Yo, Coop," my dad said, popping his head in my room.

Heart in my throat, I quickly kicked the duffel under the bed and closed up the trash bag.

"Hey, what's up, Dad?"

My dad looked down at what I was doing. "What's that?"

"What, these? Just getting rid of some old stuff," I lied. "Thinking of maybe reselling them or something to make some extra cash in case I can't find a summer job."

My dad nodded in approval. "That's what I'm talking about. Hustler spirit, got that from your old man."

"Yeah, I guess so," I said through a fake smile.

"Son, you good? You been up here all day," my dad said, stepping into the room, his smile turning to concern. The overprotective side of him taking over.

I looked at the shirt in my hand and willed myself not to break down in that moment and ask for help.

I couldn't escape the image of Mo's face when we heard the news about Jason. Horrified, scared, confused. I could tell so many thoughts and feelings were coursing through her, each one stabbing her deep. I hated seeing her like that and not being able to help.

I looked over and my dad was still staring. He wasn't letting this one go. I had to tell him something.

"Nothing, Pop, just . . . just . . . how do you tell somebody something you're afraid to tell them? If you know it's going to disappoint them?"

My dad walked over and sat down beside me, tapping my leg

for me to scoot over and make room for him. "You know you can tell me anything, right?"

I rolled my eyes. "It's not you. It's a friend."

My dad smirked. "A female friend?"

"DAD!"

"Ahh, okay, okay, I get the picture. Well, I'll tell you what I've always believed: The truth will set you free. No matter how difficult it may seem. Trust in the strength of your relationship. Believe me, I learned my lesson with your mom a long time ago."

His words sounded good. Felt good, too, and gave me the comfort I needed. He was right, I needed to tell Monique the truth. So that's what I was going to do. As terrifying as it sounded.

"Thanks, Dad."

"No problem, champ. But I came in to ask if you wanted some breakfast."

"Nah, I'm good. I got something to take care of."

"Sounds good, little man," my dad said, heading out.

When I was sure the coast was clear I put the stolen clothes away since I couldn't get rid of them now anyway, and my mind turned to bigger things.

The cops in this town didn't move that fast. Unless there was something motivating them. I couldn't help but wonder how they had pegged Jason as one of the guys behind the masks so quickly. In most cases, even hard evidence wasn't enough to get an arrest, let alone a conviction. Yet, here we were with Jason arrested within twenty-four hours of a crime I was certain he didn't commit. Something didn't smell right.

I had to figure out what really went down after we all split up.

It was day two post-riot, and I would rather have hidden away from the city that was on the hunt for Rico, Skull Face, and me. But none of this was going to go away or solve itself, so I hopped in the shower, got cleaned up, and shuffled down the stairs. I steadied my hands long enough to type out a text. Ever since the news broke, I had been on shaky ground, and apparently, my hands had taken that a little too literally.

Me: Mo, you up?

Mo: up? I haven't slept

Me: can I come over?

Mo: yea

I walked out into the sunlight and was immediately assaulted by the humidity. Despite it not even being midmorning yet, it was already baking outside, and I made a beeline for Monique's. My sliders were sticking to the asphalt and slapping back up against my heels as I walked.

Get it together, Coop, I thought, trying to shake off my anxiety.

Up ahead Monique was sitting on the porch, the morning sun hitting her in a way that made her sparkle golden.

"Mind if I join you?" I called out.

She turned to me, startled. Her eyes looked empty, so much so it scared me. I couldn't recall a time she looked like this. But who could blame her, considering everything she'd been through over the past couple days?

"Hey, Coop, yeah of course."

She stood up as I climbed the stairs, unable to meet my eyes. Instead, she wrapped her arms around me and squeezed. I pulled her close, not wanting to let go for a second. It was a long embrace, something I think we both needed. Holding her close was the only thing that felt right in the last few days.

"How you been, Coop?" she asked as we both sat down. "I feel like we haven't really spoken in a while and then I kind of dragged you into my whole mess."

I felt like such a jerk. Here Mo's brother was in jail and she was worried about me. Feeling her own guilt when I was the one who was in the wrong.

"I feel better now that I'm here with you," I blurted out. What was I thinking? I didn't want Mo to think I was hitting on her. This was no time to be professing my feelings. "I mean, I'm better than I was before I got here," I said, blushing. It was clumsy, but she knew what I was saying.

Mo nudged her shoulder into mine. "I miss you, too, Coop," she said with a slight smile. "Well come on in," she said, jumping up and stepping inside. "It's already getting hot out here."

As I followed her in and closed the door behind me, the depth of her sadness dawned on me. The curtains in her living room were still drawn, like she was trying to shut the world out. She hadn't changed out of her pajamas, and her hair was pulled back in a messy ponytail, but she was still the most beautiful girl you could ever hope to see—even in her most vulnerable state.

"How *you* holding up is the question?" I said, taking a seat on the living room couch.

"It varies from minute to minute."

"I feel you," I say, nodding in understanding.

"How could he do something so stupid?" Monique slumped onto the couch beside me.

"Do what?" I asked, not wanting to talk too much in case I gave myself away.

"Steal—loot! Whatever you want to call it!" I could feel my heart pounding in my chest and, at that moment, I was grateful that she didn't have the same BS radar as my father. Could I really tell her the truth now?

She hung her head in her hands. "I'm just"—she sighed and paused before lowering her voice—"*disappointed.*"

That word hung in the air like a thick blanket, stifling us both in the already heavy atmosphere. There was just something about the thought of disappointing the people you care about that stung a whole lot worse than their anger.

Anger meant someone still cared. Disappointment felt a lot like giving up.

But lying to her also felt like giving up. I had to come clean.

"I need to know who the other guys were behind the masks. Maybe they can provide an alibi for him or something. Do you know who else was there?" Monique asked when she finally looked up at me.

I could see tears pooling in the corners of her eyes, acting like little holographic droplets that gave the brown of her irises a hazel effect.

The conflict inside me started burning more. Now was my time to speak up. I had the information she was looking for! I could give her exactly what she needed.

I opened my mouth to speak . . . and then hesitated as my thoughts spiraled.

If information got back to the cops that I had looted with Jason, this whole thing would blow up in my face. I thought about my dad's words. *The truth will set you free.* But what happens when the truth can cost you your freedom?

"I don't," I lied.

Guilt churned in my stomach at her look of disappointment.

If only she knew all there was to be disappointed about.

Mo grabbed her laptop off the table and opened it. "Well, we can start here, then."

I looked over her shoulder. She had collected every piece of footage of the riots. Compiling all the news footage released was one thing, but she'd also collected tons of things people posted on social media.

This entire time, I'd been so relieved the news hadn't captured my face. But I didn't even think about footage from the other attendees. All the stories, lives, reels, and photos taken contained so much information, so many angles.

My relief quickly turned to fear.

"That's hella footage," I said calmly.

"I know, I went overboard. But I just wanted to make sure we weren't missing anything. Can you look through and see if there's anyone you recognize? Someone that could've been with Jason?" She handed over the laptop for me to take.

My palms were so sweaty I made sure our hands didn't touch.

I scanned back and forth between images, posts, and videos. All of it looked pretty standard, stuff I had already seen glimpses of online. That's when a video hit me like a freight train. The first thing I noticed was the duffel bag. I zoomed in. My face was covered, thankfully, but it was me, no doubt. I was even wearing the same shoes, though most people in the city had a pair of New Balance 993s, so that wasn't a big deal. I zoomed in some more and saw a dead giveaway. My bracelet I never took off.

As I stared at the image, I felt conflicted. If Mo had seen this already and recognized me, she probably would have confronted me. My instincts told me chances were high she hadn't watched every single video post she'd downloaded. And if she did, she probably didn't zoom in like I had.

Did she know about me being down there that day?

The thought was like a large bitter pill that refused to go down no matter how hard I tried to swallow it. The thought of her seeing me in the same light as her brother—the man who had put her and her mother in the position to fish him out of troubled waters—was too much for me to bear.

I did what I had to do and deleted it.

"Coop?" Mo's voice made me wince.

"Yeah?" I said, not looking up from the screen. I pretended to run through more footage, knowing full well I had already gone through that folder. But if I looked at her at that moment, she would have definitely known something was up.

"Recognize anyone?"

"Nope," I said, returning her laptop. Another lie.

Mo reeled back on the couch. "Ughhh. I wish he would just snitch," she quickly replied. The words poured from her mouth with a bitterness that I hadn't seen from her before. "There's no way he did this, but his so-called 'loyalty' is going to get him thirty to life."

That hit me like the H Street trolley. Thirty years? To life?! I would be stacked up right there beside him on the firing line if we didn't figure out what was going on—and fast, too.

"Mo, you and I both know Jay didn't do this," I started up.

"Yeah, but no one is going to believe us. I went to talk to him yesterday, but they didn't even let us see him. We just spoke to the police instead."

"What they say?"

Mo caught me up on everything that went down at the station, including the name of the victim.

"And I didn't tell you the worst part, Coop. Jason had a gun on him when they found him. No matter what, they're going to pin this on him."

There was silence in the room as we both got a handle on the situation. I thought back to the moment Rico handed Jason that gun.

One thing was for sure: Talking it out like this was making things all the more real. As painful as the slow, seeping reality of it was, it had to be done. And as much as it scared the hell out of me, it was also helping put things in perspective.

"You know what we have to do, right?" I asked as I recommitted to what I had already decided before walking through her front door that morning.

"What?"

"We have to find who really killed Melissa Davis."

Monique looked up with a fiery determination in her eyes. Now, that was a look I had seen on her before.

She grabbed her phone off the coffee table.

"What are you doing?"

"I think you're right, Coop. It's a great idea. Only thing is, I don't know the first thing about solving a crime. So I'm googling *how to solve a murder*."

I had to smile at that. Even though I had said the words, I wouldn't have known what to do next. But Mo did.

"Well, according to Google, there are two main steps. First, we need to identify our suspects—and it says murder victims, particularly women, usually know their murderer. And then we figure out who had means, access, and motive. That should lead us to the culprit."

"Oh, sounds simple," I said sarcastically.

Mo cut her eyes at me and I had to smirk.

"Since we have nothing else to go off of, maybe we can ask around the neighborhood and see if anybody knows anything about who was with him two days ago."

I could feel beads of sweat forming around my hairline.

Think, Coop, I told myself. I couldn't let her go down that path because it would lead her straight to me.

"How about you let me handle that part?" I spat out.

Mo scrunched up her face. "Tell me more."

"Well . . . ," I continued, searching for an excuse. "If *you* go around asking, people will know you're only asking to help Jay's case. Nobody will say anything because they wouldn't want to be involved. You'll scare them away. If *I* go asking, I can pass it off like I'm just, you know, getting the neighborhood gossip."

Mo squinted her eyes as if she was thinking. I wiped the top of my forehead before any beads of sweat could trickle down.

"Okay, makes sense," she said, finally giving me permission to exhale. "While you do that, I guess we need to learn more about Melissa and who she knew, who she was connected to."

"I'm wit' it," I replied coolly, trying to seem at ease even though my stomach was in knots. "Look at us, just a couple of baby sleuths."

CHAPTER SEVEN

MONIQUE
FIRST CLUE

The hours seemed to melt away as Coop and I scoured socials for details on Melissa Davis. It was the next best place to start beyond figuring out who was with Jason that day. We went through every social site known to woman and still couldn't find a trace of her anywhere—not a blog, a tag, a comment, a like, or a mention. For someone as young as her, not having a trace online was weird.

Really, it was more than weird, it was a red flag.

The light from the screen started to hurt my eyes, and as comfy as it was sitting in bed, my back was stiffening from being hunched in front of the computer.

I looked over at Coop who sat in the corner on an old lime green bean bag. It reminded me of us as kids, when we would jump off my bed and face-plant into it. Until one time Cooper missed and busted his nose. Ha! I remember holding ice to it for him and thinking we would be together forever, playing "house" in my mind. Those times were simpler.

My thoughts were interrupted when something on screen suddenly caught my attention.

"Oh snap, I think this could be her!" I shouted after spotting what looked like Melissa's Instagram profile.

Coop jumped up and stood beside the bed, awkwardly trying to crane his neck to see my screen.

"Umm, I don't bite, ya know," I said, offering him a chance to get closer to me.

I could see the wheels in his head turning. It was so cute. The reason I loved Coop so much was simply because of the person he was. Always respectful, never pressuring me, always considering how I felt. It was kind of a turn-on. Especially after some of the boys I had dealt with before. Coop finally kicked off his shoes and hopped in the bed beside me. I nestled a tiny bit closer just to make him a little more uncomfortable. Up against him I could feel his solid frame. His arms were more muscular than I remembered, and he smelled good. The heat from his body started to melt me, but I shook it off. I needed to focus.

We peered down at the screen as I clicked on Melissa's profile. The page took a second to load and my heart dropped when the next screen just showed a huge padlock.

"Ugh, it's private."

"What about her friends list—anyone we know?" Coop asked.

But that was blocked, too.

"This sucks," I said, slamming my laptop shut. I was getting frustrated.

"I saw this movie once where this lady was in a new town with no trace or background, turns out, she was in some sort of witness protection program," Coop said, breaking me out of my feelings.

"Hmm, and you think Melissa could've been?"

"I don't know. It would explain a lot. Like why someone had it out for her and why we can barely find a trace of her."

He made a pretty good point. But it didn't mean he was right. While it was a logical explanation for this whole thing, it seemed too far-fetched. A major city like DC was probably the worst place for a person to hide.

"I don't know. I will say, between the cops moving in on Jason so fast, the lack of info about her in the news and media, and the anonymous tip, something definitely feels off."

"Tip?" Coop asked, cocking his head to the side.

"Yeah, the cops said someone called in a tip on Jason, gave his description and everything. It's how they found him with the gun."

Coop looked just as perplexed as I was. The room fell silent for a second—we were both lost in our own thoughts.

"I wish we knew where she worked or lived or something," Coop said, snapping me back.

Where she lived. That gave me an idea.

"Cooper, that's it!" I said, flipping my laptop back open.

"What?"

"I think I have an idea. We've been so focused on finding her socials, but there may be something on her in, like, actual records."

"You mean like police records?"

"No, city records," I said as I showed Coop my screen. "I remember one of the stories that came out said she was killed just a couple blocks from her home."

"She lived nearby," Coop whispered.

"Not just that, they said *home*, not residence. Maybe she was a homeowner. The county tax website can pull up any homeowner in the city if you have a name and zip code, which we do. It's a longshot, but could work."

"Mo, you're a genius!" Coop shouted.

I smiled and batted my eyes, and for a brief moment I could feel the spunky piece of me that I loved so much beaming through.

"Not really, just learned this doing a class project in DC History. Guess school is actually good for something," I joked.

We watched as a list of names popped up on the screen with addresses beside them. Our eyes started to scan, line by line, looking through all the names of homeowners in a three-mile radius.

I scrolled down and down and down, until there were no names left. No Melissa.

"Hmm, it was worth a shot," I whispered, deflated.

"What zip code you put in?" Coop asked.

"Ours, 20002."

"What if you go a few blocks in the other direction? Away from H Street?"

It was a good thought. I got to typing and pulled up a map of the city with corresponding zip codes for each section.

"Let's see it looks like . . . 20510 . . . I've never even heard of that zip code. Let's check it," I said as I typed it in. A much shorter list of names popped up with addresses beside them.

After a few scrolls, we both saw it.

"Look! There's a house registered to a Melissa Davis and a Donna Brown on Second and F Street," I read aloud.

"Second is where we—" Coop started.

"We what?"

Coop just stared blankly, as if he forgot what he was going to say.

"Uh, nothing, it's just we weren't too far from there when we went to see the mayor speak."

"Oh, yeah, it's creepy, right? I wonder who Donna Brown is."

"Probably someone who has more info than us."

I looked at Coop as a heavy thought hit me. My mind had been so preoccupied with my own stuff that I didn't even think about what Melissa's family and friends must've been going through. Sure, I was torn up about Jason, but at least he was alive. Melissa might have been a wife, a sister, an aunt, maybe even a mom—she had to be someone to someone. No one is no one to no one.

"I wonder if that's Melissa's partner? Or disgruntled ex," I said. "You know almost forty percent of women murdered are killed by a partner, or some crazy statistic like that?"

"Yeah, you mentioned something like that," Coop said.

"Sorry, just fascinating."

"Nah, you right. It's good to keep in our heads. So what do we do now?" he asked.

"Only one thing *to* do. We go down there," I replied without thinking.

"You serious?" Coop looked at me like he'd never seen me before.

"I look like I'm joking?" I hit back before writing Melissa's address down and getting up. "Maybe we can get some answers from this Donna person."

"All right then," Coop said, scratching the back of his neck. "Let's go, I guess."

I jumped up and pulled a T-shirt and shorts from my dresser drawer. I turned away from Coop and slipped off my pajama shirt, exposing my hips and back all the way up to my neck. I could feel his eyes glued to me, but I didn't mind. "Okay, Cooper King, let's go."

As we left the house, I realized that as high stakes as this whole trying to solve a crime thing was, it kind of excited the hell out of me.

CHAPTER EIGHT
COOPER
BREAK-IN

My brain was spinning. The fact that someone dropped a dime on Jason set off alarms in my head. One thing Jason took pride in was being thorough. In all senses of the word. He told us to mask up for a reason. He wouldn't go against his own rule. So how could somebody ID him? And anybody who knew he was there must've known I was there, too.

As if that wasn't enough to keep my mind busy, being alone with Mo in her room certainly was. There was an energy here I couldn't quite shake. Last time I'd been here, we were both so innocent, but now, Mo was more like a woman than she was a kid. Even though her room looked exactly as I remembered when we were little. The same spelling bee medals alongside framed pictures of Mo's slam poetry performances. Everything had a place. Everything except me.

Until she invited me in her bed. *What was that?!* The sweet scent from her long, gold-tipped locks pulled me in. It was an invitation I couldn't ignore.

And before I knew what was happening, she was getting dressed in front of me! The sight of her smooth bare skin had enticed me. Her softness stirred something inside me that made me turn away. If I didn't know any better, I'd think she was flirting with me. Teasing me even.

My mind started to drift to more . . . sensual places. Until the words echoed in my head, *thirty to life*. That sobered me up real quick.

"This is us, Coop," Mo called out as the trolley came to a stop.

We got off just before the Queen Vic, a local pub where a lot of the new white people in the area hung out. Mo had her phone out with Maps open just to make sure that we landed at the right spot.

"Just a few blocks this way," she called out as we hopped off the trolley onto H Street.

The strip was still in disarray with boarded-up buildings, but somehow seemed even more active than before the riots. There were so many people milling about, snapping photos of the wreckage, documenting the scene as if it were some sort of museum of pain. Me, I kept my head down.

Ever since the riots, the police presence in the area picked up tremendously. Squad cars were everywhere. At any moment I felt like a cop could pull up and arrest me right in front of Mo. That'd be the end of me. The end of us.

When we turned off the strip, the noise settled down. The police presence subsided and I could breathe a little. The walk to Melissa's was actually pretty peaceful. For a brief moment it felt like just like any other day.

"I see you're still wearing your bracelet," Mo said out of nowhere.

"What?!" I exclaimed.

"Uh, your lucky bracelet?" she said, nodding down at my wrist.

Her words shocked me for a second. I tried to recover quickly. "Yeah, you already know," I said, my mind clouded by both thoughts of my mom and that video I deleted. I hated that I had been so deceptive.

"How's your dad been?" Mo pressed. I knew she really meant *How's your dad been since your mom died?*

"With Mom's medical bills and all the other stuff, it's been tough. But he's been good. Much better than a while back. He's been working a lot. And I can tell he's worried about me but I'm straight."

"Are you, though?"

I snapped my head in Mo's direction.

"I'm sorry. It's just you know, you kind of disappeared, Coop. The only time I would really see you was with Jason. I barely even saw you at school."

She wasn't wrong. When my mom died, I took a bit of a turn. I wouldn't say I became rebellious. I just stopped caring about anything. Maybe that's what depression feels like.

"No, I hear you. But I'm doing better now. I promise."

"Good. You know I'm always here for you, Coop. You're my person."

I smiled at that. "You're my person, too."

Mo smiled back. It was a nice moment until—

Bzzt, bzzt, bzzt

Mo's phone buzzed and she quickly whipped it out.

"Says to turn on this street and it should be on this block."

When we turned, we saw a row of houses across from a huge, stately building.

"Welp, there it is," Mo said as we stared up at the modest two-story row home. The brick was painted white with black accents and looked nicely renovated like most of the homes in the area. But the yard was slightly unkempt, which made the house stand out among the other well-manicured lawns.

We waited outside in silence for a good couple of minutes. We had left Mo's so fast that we hadn't stopped to think what we would actually do when we got here.

I looked around the street. We were a few blocks from where Jason and I had looted. It was eerie. I imagined Melissa running for her life, trying with all her might to make it back home. Maybe she ran like I did, desperately, until her lungs burned and her legs felt like lead weights. I wondered what went through her mind before it all went black. Did she see the door to her home before she died? Did she feel a flicker of hope before the—nothingness?

Mo walked right up to the building and knocked.

"Mo!" I hissed.

"What," she hissed back. "Get over here."

I scanned the street to see if anyone was watching us, much like I had as the lookout for Jason. If there was one way to land myself in a steel chair for questioning, this was it.

"I'm coming!"

Mo knocked again and rang the doorbell, but there was only silence.

"I don't think anyone's home," I whispered.

"Why are you whispering? We aren't doing anything wrong . . . yet."

I slowly turned to Mo, my head cocked to the side. "What do you mean *yet*?"

"I mean, we didn't come all this way for nothing. At least I didn't," Mo said in a muffled voice.

"Mo, why are *you* whispering?"

Mo stared daggers at me, daring me to back down. I rubbed my hands on the back of my neck. We were walking a fine line. She didn't know what I knew. That if I were tied to the looting *and* breaking into the victim's house, I'd probably hurt Jason's case much more than I'd help it.

Mo's brow furrowed, accentuating the little scar just under her eyebrow she got when we were kids down at Stanton Park. We had been racing down a footpath when she tripped and fell headfirst into a small rock protruding from the dirt. I carried her the quarter mile back to her house.

I thought the scar was badass, but I knew what that look meant. Before I could act, Mo headed to the side of the house where a gate was open.

I looked around the property to see if there were any cameras. None I could spot. I groaned as I followed.

"Mo, we can't just break in. Let's maybe just check the trash cans to see what we can learn, like they do in the movies."

"Ew, gross! You can check the trash cans; I'm going to see if there's anything else I can find."

I couldn't help but admire Mo's spirit. The truth of the matter was I needed her more than she needed me.

"Cooper!" she said just loud enough to rattle me. "Look."

Up ahead, a back window of the house was open.

"What do you think?"

I thought about everything on the line. As much as I was terrified to get myself in more trouble, I knew it had to be all or nothing if we were going to prove Jason's innocence. And my own.

"Uhh, let's do it," I said unsure. "But we need to hurry. Donna could be back any minute."

"Noted. Three minutes," Mo said, already climbing into the home. I followed, and when I reached out to hoist myself up, I instantly felt tiny glass particles in the window pane, not quite sharp enough to break skin. Once inside I stared down at my palm and picked out a few tiny shards. I looked back at the window and realized it wasn't open. It was busted out. That wasn't a good sign.

I drew the curtains for cover. If anyone saw us, they'd likely call the police and we definitely didn't need those problems. I dusted my palm and Mo did the same.

"Someone was here already." I pointed out the busted windows to Mo.

"Oh snap, you're right. Good stuff, detective," Mo teased. "Who do you think would've done that?"

Mo and I locked eyes and I could tell by how her face hardened we had the same thought.

"The murderer?" she muttered, answering her own question.

"Very likely. Probable even."

"Okay, maybe you were right, let's make this quick."

"Two and a half more minutes."

Mo nodded as she crept through the quiet house. The hair on the back of my neck stood at attention. If a murderer was breaking into Melissa's house, that meant they knew each other and it definitely wasn't a spur of the moment crime committed by Jason as police suspected. A small part of me had started to believe there was little hope in freeing Jason, but this was just the boost I needed.

I picked up the first thing I saw, a photo of Melissa. Mo looked at me and didn't need to say a word, we were thinking the same thing. We were in the right place.

"Let's split up," Mo said.

"Yeah, don't leave any fingerprints, either," I replied.

Mo tilted her head. "Yes, sir. Although I'm pretty sure the police can only compare your fingerprints or DNA to others already on their files."

"Oh," I said, only slightly embarrassed. "I knew that."

"Suuurrre you did. I'll go this way."

Mo walked off and I just stood stunned, smitten really. I shook the feeling off and tried to focus up—we had work to do.

Melissa's house was so neat and put together. It seemed like she hadn't been there in days, even before her tragic demise. As I paced through the home, it hit me. This was the second time within a week that I had broken into a building, and both times had been because of a Simms sibling.

Mo didn't spare a second. She combed through that house like a pro, much like Jason combing through that store we looted. If I hadn't known any better, I would have thought she knew what she was looking for.

I tried to imagine what might be a giveaway sign that someone wanted it out for Melissa. *A past-due bill? A threatening letter?*

But the more I looked around, the more this just seemed like a normal home. Maybe Melissa Davis wasn't in witness protection or part of some underground scene. Maybe she was just in the wrong place at the wrong time.

Ninety more seconds.

A car drove past outside and I nearly jumped out of my socks. My feet started to itch, but Mo wasn't going anywhere anytime soon. She moved from room to room like a real sleuth. If patience is a virtue, I sure wasn't feeling all that virtuous.

"Mo, let's hurry up. Donna could show up any minute!"

"Almost done, Coop. We might as well check every room; we're already here."

"Fine. Thirty seconds!"

I made my way back down the hallway and through the kitchen, randomly checking the drawers. I opened and started to close one until something caught my eye that brought me back to myself. *Whoa . . .*

It was the insignia that I had seen on the pamphlet in Jay's room. It was on a piece of paper wedged in the back of the drawer and . . . if I . . . could just . . .

It was wedged pretty tight.

I looked around for a second, willing my brain to find a way to release the trapped piece of paper. Mo was right, we had already broken into the place. Who cared if we roughed it up a little? Melissa wouldn't.

I planted my feet and gave the drawer a really hard tug to yank it off the tracks.

But it wasn't enough.

I yanked harder, twisting and pulling the drawer until it popped out and the papers in the back came out with it.

In all, there were four copies of the same pamphlet—the same one I'd found in Jay's bedroom with the words THE TIME IS NOW written in huge letters across the front alongside the image of some sort of beast. Before I had a chance to even process what this could mean—

Crash!

Mo slid out the bedroom on her heels and stared at me, confirming that it was neither of us who had done something to cause that sound. It came from upstairs. And I was suddenly afraid that whoever had broken that window hadn't left.

My heart started to pound as I thought about going for one of the steak knives on the kitchen counter. *Don't panic. Maybe it was just Donna*, I tried to tell myself. But the tiny shards of glass from earlier wouldn't let me be that optimistic. Just before I grabbed the steak knife, I looked over to Mo and she was ferociously waving her hand at me, calling me over to her.

She must have seen a way out.

I decided against the weapon and made a run for it as the unmistakable thuds of large footsteps coming down the stairs and through the living room reverberated through the house. By the time I took the corner, Mo was already halfway inside a small closet, beckoning me to follow. We barely had time to close the door before the stranger appeared in the doorway of the office.

The closet was tight and stuffy, filled with the scent of old jackets. I watched through the narrow gap between the closet door and its frame as the intruder entered the room. They had a bulky figure, but I couldn't make out their face.

I bit my lip, debating whether to push the door open just a little more to get a better look. But Mo was shaking her head, like she knew what I was thinking.

I looked out to the intruder, who moved with an air of cautious purpose and intensity, and decided against pushing our luck. I thought back to the busted window.

Had they been here the whole time? They must've.

Perhaps we'd walked right into a trap.

My heart raced as they scanned the room, and Monique clenched my hand so hard her nails dug into my skin. It was impossible to tell whether the newcomer was a friend or foe, but I prayed they wouldn't discover us.

I started to think of all the scenarios. If anything, I could rush the person, catch them off guard, and knock them down. It would at least allow enough time for Mo to get away, although she probably wouldn't leave me.

I felt around the closet for a weapon, or at least something I could use to fend the person off. Next to my feet was a small black box with a smooth handle. As carefully as I could, I kneeled down to pick it up. I guess my movement surprised Mo because she yanked on my hand, rustling one of the jackets.

I jerked from the mouth of the door and Mo and I pressed our bodies against the back of the closet, behind the garments that hung in there.

We held our breath as the stranger's heavy steps approached the closet. Mo pressed her free hand to her mouth to stifle any sound. I started to raise the black box, just in case I needed to swing it.

The shadow of the stranger appeared in the closet door; a black leather glove reached for the doorknob. My heart pounded so loudly in my chest that I was afraid they could hear it.

And just as their fingers brushed against the closet door . . . the sound of sirens wailed in the distance. The hand quickly darted away, and the intruder abandoned their pursuit, clearing the room and disappearing down the hallway.

Monique and I waited a moment to ensure they were gone. When we knew the coast was clear, we practically tripped over each other running from our hiding place. Before I knew it Mo was already headed out the window and I was right behind her. But right at the window I couldn't jump out for some reason. In fact, I couldn't move at all. I looked to my shoulder and saw the black glove gripping my shirt tight.

I was caught.

CHAPTER NINE

COOPER
THE TIME IS NOW

My consciousness seemed to teleport back to the moment I collided with the cop after the protest shooting. I remember my heartbeat, a frenzied drum that made me feel like my chest would explode. My palms slick with sweat, my breaths shallow and uneven. The overwhelming urge to run, the hairs on my neck at full attention. The memory came rushing back because I felt that feeling all over again when I saw that hand on my shoulder.

They say when animals sense danger they can go into fight, flight, freeze, or fawn mode. Luckily, I went into flight.

"Get off me!" I yelled, ripping my shoulder away as hard as I could, the black box from the closet still in my hand. The force of it made me tumble out the window with a *thud*. Thankfully it wasn't a long fall.

When I looked back to the house, the mystery man was already gone.

Then I searched for Mo and realized I was wrong about her. She'd totally abandoned me under pressure!

The wind whipped my face as I ran down Second Street, and

pretty soon, I saw Mo up ahead. Buildings were no more than blurry outlines as my eyes watered and every muscle in my body thumped. I didn't know who was in Melissa's house or what they were doing there, but I did know one thing: They may have seen my face.

This is why Jason always says to mask up.

Not that it had done him any good. Still, if that person was Melissa's killer and they did actually see our faces, or at least mine, life was going to get a whole lot trickier and the cops would become the least of our worries.

Once we made it back to Mo's, we both collapsed on the floor of the basement, rolled onto our backs, and just looked up at the ceiling. That ceiling fan, spinning for dear life.

The only audible sounds in the room must have been our own heartbeats and labored breathing. I kept my eyes closed for as long as I could, feeling the sweat on my forehead begin to drip onto my eyelids. I didn't move. I didn't want to think about this situation anymore. I just wanted to exist and be perfectly still, with Mo.

But soon I heard her start to stir, and the squeak of her sneaker against the floor as she pulled herself up made me wince.

If only I could stay hidden here forever.

"Coop?"

Her voice cut through the air and I winced again. I could see that black glove on my shoulder in my mind's eye. I could hear the gunshots at the protest. I could feel the weight of the duffel bag full of stolen clothes eating into my shoulder. It was all too much.

"COOP?" Mo asked, louder this time.

When I opened my eyes, Mo was already sitting up with her knees pulled to her chest and her arms wrapped around them.

"You good?" she asked.

"Yeah—you?"

"I'm okay."

I waited a moment.

"They saw me."

"Who?"

"Whoever that was. They grabbed me and I managed to get them off."

Monique stared at me stunned, then stood up abruptly. I didn't know where she was going, but I hung my head as my heart rate slowed down. With every breath I took, it became steadier until, eventually, it was back to normal.

"Here," Mo said.

I looked up and saw her holding a glass of water above my head. Just what I needed. I reached up and thanked her before taking a long swig from that glass. I felt the cool liquid make its way down the back of my throat and, surprisingly, it calmed me right down. For the first time since we'd made a break for it, I was able to string a thought together.

The first question that sprung to mind was, obviously, who was that person? More importantly, what did they want from Melissa?

"Do you think that was Donna?"

"Not a chance. Definitely a man."

"What do you think they were doing there?" Mo asked.

"Gloves on, they weren't there for nothing good. That plus the broken window, I think it's a good chance that was our shooter."

"If so, that's great! That would mean it couldn't be Jason." There was a genuine happiness in her voice that told me she may have considered the possibility Jason was guilty. I wondered if deep down, I was thinking the same thing. "I feel like we haven't the first clue about who that could be. If only we'd found another clue at Melissa's place . . ."

Mo's words made me realize I had completely forgotten about the pamphlets I'd grabbed at Melissa's. I saw them sticking out of my pocket, and then my eyes wandered to my hands and I felt a mixture of shock and excitement.

The small box from Melissa's closet was still in my hand. In all the commotion, I had taken it with me. Upon examining it, I saw it had a small lock on the front that I tugged at but couldn't budge.

That was a problem for later. In the meantime, I pulled the pamphlets from my pocket and read over them again. There was no mistake. These were the same as those on Jay's table.

"I think," I replied, "these might be . . . a clue."

"Where'd you get those?"

"They were jammed in a kitchen drawer."

"I think I've seen that before," Mo said as she walked over to me. I handed her one and she wandered slowly toward the basement door again.

Mo grabbed the pamphlet off Jay's table and held them up for both of us to see. The ones from Melissa's apartment were a little different; maybe newer, by the look of them. But the tagline and insignia were most definitely the same. Just as I had thought.

THE TIME IS NOW.

Time for what? Maybe this wasn't just related to the riot.

"Why would they both have this? You think it ties them together?" Mo asked.

"I mean, there's no way this is just a coincidence. Right?"

We both went quiet as the thought settled in. Just moments ago, I'd been more sure than ever Jason couldn't have been the triggerman. But now, with the possibility of a connection between Jason and Melissa, things were just . . . confusing.

But I could tell neither of us wanted to think about that connection right now, so I changed gears. "I took this from Melissa's, too," I said, lifting the black box. "It's locked, though."

I brushed it aside as Mo sat back down in front of the computer and opened up an incognito window.

"Okay, you work on opening that box while I look up our only firm suspect: Donna Brown."

"You think she could really be a suspect?"

"Gotta be. Wouldn't be the first time roommates beefed to the point of murder. Could've even been her partner; we just don't know."

As Mo searched online, I played around with the locked box. The thing was sturdy, its metal surface cold to the touch. I ran my fingers over its edges, searching for any vulnerabilities. My mind raced as I recalled every heist movie I'd ever seen, and every trick and technique I'd learned from the streets.

I glanced around the dimly lit basement, searching for something, anything, that could help me crack this mystery open. My eyes landed on a worn-out toolbox tucked away under Jason's desk.

Bingo.

I walked over and grabbed a sturdy-looking screwdriver out the box. I positioned the tip of the screwdriver in the seam of the lock, pressing down with just enough force, but it wouldn't quite give.

I took a deep breath, gave a determined twist and . . . *click.*

The screwdriver bit into the lock. It resisted at first, but I persisted, feeling the lock give way slowly. I gave one final yank and the lock finally snapped and the lid of the box creaked open.

I wasn't prepared for what I saw next.

"What the—" Mo let out in her own corner. "Coop, come here!"

My jaw still on the ground, I picked up the box and walked over to Mo. There on the computer was a picture of Melissa Davis with a group of other people. She looked to be our age at the time, so it must be a few years old. She was standing with classmates, all of them with suits on.

It looked like a pretty ordinary photo. I was missing something.

"That's Melissa."

Mo clicked on the photo and it took her to an article.

She scrolled down to the picture and put her cursor over the caption.

"Yes, exactly. But this is what comes up when you search Donna. According to the caption, this person is Donna Brown, *not* Melissa Davis."

"Maybe they were in Street Law or whatever together so they're both in the pic."

"But Melissa's name isn't here! C'mon, Coop."

I understood, but I didn't. All these discoveries one after another were playing with my head.

"Wait . . . so you're saying . . . Melissa and Donna . . . are the same person?" I asked.

"YES! That would explain why Melissa barely had a trace online—she isn't a real person! It was just an alias. I mean there's barely any trace of Donna, either, except this. But why, though?" Mo asked out loud.

I looked down into the small black box at what I'd found and the pieces started to click slowly but surely.

"Mo," I said.

"Yeah?"

I picked up the silver badge from the box and held it out for Mo to see.

"I think she was a cop."

CHAPTER TEN

MONIQUE
THE SPHINX

The nights seemed to get longer and longer with each passing day, and I was starting to hate the darkness. I just couldn't find solace in the silence anymore. It was the one time of day when my thoughts wouldn't quiet down because there was nothing else to do. The only time I'd actually sleep was when my body caved in out of exhaustion.

I must have passed out at some point the night before, though, because I woke up with my phone practically glued to the side of my face. I had been talking things through with Coop until I feel asleep. Cooper, the one bright spot in all of this.

At least we now had a firm clue to dig deeper on: Melissa and Donna were one and the same.

Why hadn't the news mentioned Donna was a cop? Why were they using her alias?

There was so much we didn't know about this woman. What blew my mind was that the only explanation I could think of was that she'd been so deep undercover there was no going back. I wasn't even sure if that was a thing.

I sat up and looked at my reflection in Jason's full-length

mirror. I looked exactly how I felt, and the imprint on my cheek was about to start aching.

I missed Jason so much I'd started sleeping in his basement. Around him I always felt safe, and with him out of the house, I was feeling as vulnerable as ever.

As I stared into the mirror, I noticed a black duffel bag strap in the corner of the room. Curiosity got the best of me. I found a bag full of clothes.

All the clothes still had the tags on them, expensive clothes that I knew Jason must've stolen. The police weren't lying. Not only had he been at the protest, he was one of the rioters. Which I already had suspected, but the confirmation still stung.

I felt sad and mad to my bones.

"Monique?" Mom called, startling me. "Come on and eat, honey. We gotta get ready."

"Coming," I called back.

I grabbed the bag to take it up to my room. Just in case the cops came looking, I didn't want them to find it. And I couldn't let my mom know what I'd found. It'd destroy her. She was already beside herself, and any extra info would send her over the edge. I had to face this alone. Or at least with Coop by my side.

I was so glad he was in the trenches with me on this because I didn't think I could do this alone. Spending so much time with him again reminded me of the crush I'd always had on him and the chemistry we had. He was supporting me emotionally, but part of me wanted him to comfort me physically, too. But I feared that may make things complicated.

I tried to turn my thoughts to what was going to happen

today. The fact that Jay got clearance for visitors had to be a good sign. I needed to find the connection between him and Donna and the only way to do that was to talk to Jay in person and ask the questions that needed to be asked. Whether I liked the answers Jason would give was a whole other story.

I was afraid of asking Jay, straight up, if he knew Donna. And if he'd killed her. I was even more afraid of what his answer might be.

I made my way to the kitchen after stashing the stolen clothes in my closet and was hit with the smell of bacon and eggs. I had to stifle a gag. Being on the fumes of sleep and waking up riddled with anxiety had me feeling like I was about to hurl. But I knew how much it annoyed Mom when food went to waste, so I took a deep breath and focused on putting one foot in front of the other. There was already a plate on the table for me, so I fixed it with an egg and a single slice of toast before walking out and into the living room.

Mom had the news on again. Only this time, they weren't saying much about the shooting or Melissa Davis. It was almost as if they were trying to just sweep it under the rug. That or they didn't care much about reporting on it any longer and instead found new ways to antagonize, fear-monger, or disturb their viewers.

"That all you eating?" Mom asked me as I sat down with my plate.

"Yeah, I can't seem to eat much lately."

She was silent for a second before turning to me and saying, "I don't blame you, baby. But just get something in you. I'm worried enough about your brother. Don't need you getting sick on me, you hear?"

"Yes, Momma," I said as I tucked into my first bite of toast.

Sunlight filtered through the kitchen window. I hadn't stopped to notice little things like that since this all started. And I couldn't help thinking about Jay and whether or not he'd be able to see the sun ever again. It killed me to think of him in a cold room with hardly any warmth from the outside, COs and police harassing him.

I shook the thought off and put a determined look on my face. *If anyone can figure this out, it's you,* I thought to myself.

We hopped in the car and headed to southeast DC—more specifically, 1901 D Street.

"You nervous?" my mom asked.

I was, but not for the reason my mom was thinking. I couldn't get it out of my mind that Jason and Melissa were connected somehow. But what scared me more was my mother being caught off guard or shocked if the info came out during our meet with Jason. I couldn't bear seeing her in such pain. So I did what I thought was right. I told her what Coop and I had discovered about Melissa being a fake name for an undercover cop.

"Mm-hmm, you and Cooper, huh?" my mom said with a telling grin. "Well, I think you and Cooper have been watching too many dang movies."

"Ma, you have to listen to me; it's real," I said, sitting up in my seat. I couldn't tell her that we literally had Donna's badge in our house, but I needed to convince her somehow. "Her real name was Donna. Donna Brown. And we think her and Jason may have known each other, which is why they went after him so hard and fast. Don't ask how, just know we're trying to find out all we can to help Jason beat this."

My mom's jaw almost hit the steering wheel.

"Sweetie, if what you're saying is true, this is . . . way deeper and more complicated than I thought. And the cops know a whole lot more than what they're telling us. I need to know what she was undercover for. What could she have been investigating that involved Jason?"

It was the exact question that needed answering. What had Jason gotten mixed up with?

"I agree, but I also feel like we can't trust the cops. Talking to them could hurt Jason more than help."

"I think you're right, sweetie," my mom said, her wheels turning. "The reason they didn't mention her undercover status probably has to do with the fact that the investigation around her murder is still ongoing. Plus, if she *was* investigating something—or someone—big, naming her as anyone other than her alias on public television would blow everything out of the water."

"Look at you, Momma. A regular old gumshoe," I joked, but I was genuinely amazed at her ability to piece things together so quickly. It made the most sense out of any of the theories that Coop and I had come up with.

"Come on now, you know where you get your smarts from, baby girl," she said with a smirk.

I smiled. It was good to see a break in her sadness, a glimpse of her old self. The lines at the corners of her eyes hadn't curled up like that in a minute and I was glad to bring her some relief.

"Jay, too," I added cautiously as I glanced at her.

"Yeah." She sighed heavily. "I just don't know where things went wrong with your brother. I did my best, didn't I?"

She had done more than her best. She held down the fort for us and been our rock through every storm. Not only was she strong, but she was also soft, delicate, and loving. She was the mother you could run to when you made a mistake, and she would help you fix it—no questions asked. She was humble yet confident and demure yet powerful all at the same time. We hit the jackpot with her as a mother and I only wish that she could see it that way.

But she didn't. If I knew her—and I really did—she was being harder on herself than anyone else.

"You did more than your best, Mom."

She looked over at me and I offered her the best baby-girl smile I could.

As we pulled up to the front of the beige and brown building with its algae-stained windowpanes, my heart fluttered a little. This was the first time we'd be seeing Jay since the incident, and I was both nervous and excited. When we got out of the car, Mom grabbed hold of my hand and I squeezed it before interlinking our arms.

Everything else moved at lightning speed thereafter. By the looks of the horde of other people waiting to enter, this seemed like this was a general visitation day.

Checking into the prison was one of the most degrading processes I have ever experienced. Guards searched all through our possessions. Patted us down, touching me in ways I didn't think were necessary. Some folks were even asked to remove their socks, shoes, and clothing for searching. And do you want to know the saddest part of it all?

I would do it again if it meant I got to see and support my brother at his lowest moment.

Still, I felt a huge sense of relief after it was over. When we got into the visitation hall, and the heavy metal door clanged shut behind us, I noticed that there were steel tables in rows. Each one was far enough apart from the other that physical contact could be averted if one of the prisoners tried something, but it wasn't like it was the most private setting. I could hear the chatter of conversations between loved ones, but my focus was on Jay.

He looked up at us and feigned a smile, but there was a twitch—a subtle tremor that betrayed his fear. His eyes darted nervously from me to Mom and then back to me.

I walked briskly toward him and he stood up. Clearly, this was something that the guards frowned upon because they started closing in, so I froze and looked back at Mom for some sort of backup.

"Sit down," Mom mouthed to him.

He did and they backed off a little.

I reached for the top frame of one of the chairs and pulled at it, but it didn't budge. For a moment, I thought it was caught on something, but I looked down and quickly realized that they were all bolted to floor, just like the table. Then I saw it: Jay's foot shackled to the table. It wasn't his face or the fact that he was in an orange jumpsuit that sent me. It was the image of him being chained like an animal.

"He's not a murderer," I said to the guard standing closest to him. "And he is not an animal."

"Ayo, Mo, chill," Jay said. "It's okay. Just sit."

I recognized his voice but not the tone in it. It was a mix between fear and panic. Something had changed in him after just days of being in this place. I stared at him, still trying to figure out if the man before me was my brother—my cocky, loud, proud, and tough brother.

I must have looked like a fool with my head cocked and my face all twisted because Mom walked up behind me, said, "Fix your face, baby," and sat down. "How are you doing?" she asked Jay.

"I'm all right, Momma," he replied, keeping his eyes down.

"All right?" she asked. "This your version of 'all right'?"

"Momma, c'mon now. Let's not do this," he pleaded. "Not here."

Now, Mom was usually the one we all ran to. Even kids who weren't her own came to her for advice when they had messed up and were on the verge of trouble. But this time, something was different about the way she was talking. The intonation in her voice had shifted and I could have sworn I saw Jay's fear gear up a level.

Yes, Mom was cool, kind, and collected, but she also had a side to her that would put even that big, burly guard at the window to shame.

We held our breath as she decided which Momma would come out to play, and then she said, "Fine."

Finally, Jay lifted his chin and looked us in the face. His right eye had a dark circle around it and his cheek was swollen and bruised. Mom put a hand to her mouth.

"Jay, what happened?!" I asked.

"Good to see you, too, Mo," he said as he looked over to me.

"I'm sorry . . . I just, your . . ."

"It's okay," he said again, firmly looking at me and Mom. "It happens. I'm good."

Mom and I looked at each other and decided to stay strong, for Jay.

"You're right," I said. "I'm so happy to see you. I just want you out of here. In fact, I brought something for you."

I reached in my pocket, pulled out the poem I'd written for him, and slid it across the table as discreetly as I could.

"Thank you, baby sis," he said, stuffing it in his pants. "What you been up to?"

"Trying to figure out how you got into this mess."

Jason paused then shook his head. "I really don't know what happened to that woman. You have to believe me."

"We believe you. Did you know her? Donna?"

Jay's eyes got big as he shook his head and dropped his chin to his chest. I couldn't tell if he was holding back tears or thinking about what to say next.

"You've got to tell us everything you know right now," Momma said. "I don't care what kind of trouble you've gotten yourself into. I don't care if you've lied, stolen, cheated. None of that matters and I'm not going to look at you any different. We'll get you out of here."

"I don't think you can, Momma," Jay replied.

"Mom is right. The cops don't want to clear your name," I whispered. "We're your only shot. But if you keep your lips shut, you're going to rot in here." I felt bad when the words left my lips, but it was the plain truth, no point in hiding it.

I could see Jay tussling with his conscience. I thought he might never speak up and the clock at the back of the room was becoming an awfully loud reminder of the fact that we only had a few minutes left with him.

"Do you have any idea who might have had it out for you?" Mom asked. "They say they received an anonymous tip that you were the person they should be looking for."

"I don't know, Ma. I ain't done nothing to nobody!" he cried out.

Jay dropped his gaze again and turned sheepish. Something about the way he responded when I'd asked him about Donna told me he knew more than he was saying. He was hiding something—something big. I didn't want to think that, but it was a thought I couldn't control.

"Jay, you can tell us anything. We're the good guys here," I pleaded.

"I can't say too much. Windows have ears around here."

I looked at the guard who was posted up against a window near us and understood the message loud and clear.

"What does 'the time is now' mean, Jay?"

A flash of a smirk crossed Jay's face.

"You always were the smart one, baby sis. Now you're asking the right questions. I'll write you when I can, but in the meantime, follow the *sphinx*," he said.

"Visitation is over!" a voice boomed from the far end of the room.

"What?" Mom protested. "It's only been about ten minutes!"

But the officers ignored her. Instead, they grabbed Jay by the armpits, as rough as they could to show us who was in charge.

"Follow the sphinx," Jay repeated as he was stood up . The officers carted him off and just like that, he was gone.

CHAPTER ELEVEN
COOPER
SUSPECTS

I checked the time, 9 a.m.

Mo would be heading downtown to see Jay right about now and I couldn't sit still. Discovering that Jason and Donna were likely connected had sent me into a tailspin I needed to hide from her. One second I felt like Jason was innocent, then the next I was . . . unsure.

My life was riding on a decision Jason had or hadn't made and that terrified me. Two things my mom had always told me:

1. Actions have consequences.
2. Make your own choices.

For the millionth time since this whole thing began, I thought about how me getting into trouble would disappoint my mom. How my dad would be riddled with guilt that he hadn't taken care of me in the way my mom would've wanted, and the sadness that his family was gone. The thoughts made my stomach turn.

I went back to what Mo had said when we first started our . . . investigation. We needed suspects. So far, we had Jay and the mystery man who grabbed my shoulder at Donna's house. So basically, we had nothing.

Think, Cooper, think. What do you remember?

Like Mo suggested initially, we needed to take stock of everyone involved. The other members of the crew who'd looted with me and Jason. Rico and Skull Face. Mo had keyed in on them, but to keep my secret from Mo, I had to do this part by myself.

Where were they? They had to know something, anything that could help us solve this thing. But I hadn't seen either since Jay got bagged by the boys in blue, and I thought of something my pops had told me my freshman year of high school.

There's no honor among thieves. You remember that anytime you think these streets have anything but a box to offer you. Pine or steel.

I had to come up with an action plan. I couldn't let Mo do all the thinking, especially considering that could lead her down a trail to my involvement.

I needed to find a way to track down Skull Face and Rico. And as I was getting dressed that morning, and the bag of stolen clothes peeked out from under my bed, an idea hit me. I remembered the app that Jay told me about: THR1FT.

For one thing, I needed to get rid of these clothes. If Mo or Dad, or even worse, the police, found them in here, I would be in a world of hurt. But for another, it was the only way I could think of to possibly locate Skull Face or Rico. I may not have known where they were, but I remembered some of the items we swiped from the store. Maybe, just maybe, I could use the app to track them down.

I downloaded the app and made a fake account that I hoped

couldn't be traced back to me. Next, I snapped a couple of pics of the items I had and posted them on the app at a discounted rate. Then, I started hunting for THR1FTers in my location. The good thing about apps like this is that the algorithm will send you results based on your search history, purchase history, or posting history. Since I had just posted a whole bunch of stuff that was similar to the other guys' hauls, it would probably lead me right to them. Plus, I was able to filter my results to a five-mile radius.

I didn't have to wait very long for the app to prove me right. As I scrolled my feed, a shot of a vintage pair of Air Force 1s popped up less than a mile away. A pair I know was at the store we looted. I clicked on the profile pic but it was blank.

"Man . . . ," I muttered to myself. The good thing was I'd recognize Skull Face and Rico if I saw them. The bad thing was I had no guarantee that the anonymous profile belonged to either. But then again, at this point, there weren't many other options so I decided to move forward with setting up an exchange.

I knew one of the jackets I had on me was worth at least a grand on the street and his sneakers were asking $750. If he used the app right and wanted some cash as bad as I thought he did, he would accept the exchange I was about to offer him. I shot him a message, offering the jacket for his sneakers.

Then I waited . . .

. . . and waited.

Bzzt, bzzt . . .

New Inbox Message from user D1.

Gotcha, I thought.

D1: yo, you wanna trade your OW for these Nikes?

Me: Yeah. You still got 'em? I have a collector.

D1: 4sho cuzzo. Where you wanna meet up?

For some reason, my thoughts flashed to when Mo and me used to play at Stanton Park as kids.

Me: Stanton Park?

D1: bet—1 hour?

Me: I'll be there.

Growing up in the city, I had to accept that there was a slight possibility that homie—whether he was Skull Face, Jay, or some rando—might set me up to rob me. I hated that I was prejudging him; I was sounding like my pops. But I knew I needed to carry protection. So I grabbed a small canister of mace my dad kept in the kitchen drawer, just in case.

I hoped I wasn't wasting my time and would come back to Mo with something concrete. I would just need to find a way to hide how I got the information in the first place.

Within thirty minutes, messages about the clothes started to roll in. People were even offering me over asking. I had the potential to make good money and I would have to decide whether I really wanted to flip these threads or not. But not that very second.

With twenty minutes to go until the exchange, I left and headed in Stanton's direction. I wanted to get there early and scope the scene.

Stepping out into the daylight, I felt anticipation hanging in the air. There was something electric about it—I felt a charge wash over me as I looked up at the sky, which was painted with scattered clouds. The day was the coolest it'd been all summer and the breeze was just what I needed to stay calm. No doubt today was going to come with its own set of risks.

What if the other guys got nabbed, too? Then an even more terrifying possibility popped into my head. *What if I was talking to a cop and this was some kind of sting?*

But it was too late to turn back.

As I neared the park, I thought of ways to keep myself hidden from whoever was walking up. I took comfort in the fact that I had the upper hand, but I still had to confirm the person was Skull Face or Rico. Then, if it *was one of them*, I had to get what info I could out of him.

I hopped off the trolley near Petco, walked the four blocks down Seventh Street, and hung a right on Maryland. I could see the footpath and the little brown board on the bench.

HELP US KEEP YOUR PARK CLEAN!

The leaves overhead rustled as my feet hit the path. It felt ominous—like something out of an old horror movie and my gut told me to run. I could just disappear. Just leave Pops a note and get out of town. I didn't want to end up like Samir. Or Tamir Rice, another kid killed in a park much like this one. The knot that I had felt in my stomach when I collided with the cop at the riot was back and alarm bells were screeching in my mind.

Man up! I told myself. It's what Jason would've told me. *There is nowhere to run.*

With each step, the weight of the moment settled in. The tension in my body was wound so tight that I might have swung on anyone who walked up behind me.

> Me: I'll be near the monument.

I would, in fact, be as far away from it as possible but still close enough for me to see whoever approached it. I just had to hope that this guy didn't have the same plan as me.

The intermittent sunlight played hide-and-seek with the clouds as I waited and it started to look as if it might rain. The meeting time came and went. Still, no one showed. Apart from a bunch of tourists and an old lady walking her pug.

I waited a whole extra twenty minutes before giving up. I felt so defeated as I emerged from my hiding spot, wanting to kick myself for thinking I could outsmart a street cat like the one I was likely dealing with. My stakeout was a bust.

I made my way to the monument to make sure there wasn't anyone patiently waiting for me out of view. Again, no one was there. I checked the app and my message was definitely read. I thought about typing another one out to ask where they were, but then I heard—

"It's Cooper, right? Jason's li'l homie?"

I spun around to face a tall, light-skinned dude towering above me. He was posted up on the tree smoking a Black & Mild. My heart went into my throat as I recognized Skull Face. But there was a coldness about his eyes that hadn't been there before.

"Dane," he said, pointing to himself.

Suddenly, the memory of Jay speaking to this guy came

rushing back in. I heard Jay call him D. Now things were starting to fall into place. It explained his THR1FT handle, too.

"Yeah. What's good, bro? What you doing here?" I asked, feigning surprise.

"I'm supposed to meet someone for a trade," he said, eyeing my backpack. "It's not you, is it?"

"Nah. I'm just passing through, headed to the courts, shoot a few."

I stepped closer to Dane, thinking of ways to ease into the conversation. But all I could think of to say was—

"Yo, you heard what happened to Jason?"

"Aye, man. Keep your voice down," he said, swiveling his head to scope out potential eavesdroppers.

"My bad," I whispered, tapping my hand on my chest. "Have you, though? They saying some wild stuff about him."

"Of course. Who hasn't. Shit was all over the news."

An eerie pause fell between us. There was an elephant in the room and we both knew it.

"I wonder what happened?" I said aloud. Fishing. "I heard a witness ID'd him."

"I don't know nothing about that and I don't want to know. All I know is Jason is cooked, and I don't want no parts of it. Ain't nobody trying to get caught up in no murder case."

I was shocked by his answer. This was supposed to be Jason's friend and he'd already written him off as guilty. I needed to know what he knew.

"You think I wanna get caught up in it?" I said, trying to act cool but feeling anything but. "I'm just trying to protect myself. What if the cops figure out what we both know?"

Dane stepped even closer to me, pulling up his pants. I braced myself for a potential altercation. I didn't mean for my words to sound like a threat, but they totally did.

"What you tryna say, li'l homie? You sound like a fed," Dane shot at me.

"Nah, not at all," I said, throwing my hands up in defense. "I'm just trying to figure out what happened to my man. I'm surprised you not," I shot back. "Look, if anything we need to stick together and tell each other what we know. We were all there."

Dane cocked his head to the side and twisted his face at me. He snorted and fell back as he shook his head, contemplating something. He looked around one last time before turning to me.

"You didn't hear this from me, but I can't speak for where Jason was that day. One minute we were running to the bus as planned, and the next I looked back and he was nowhere in sight. I wasn't sticking around. I hopped on the bus and got the fuck."

"That's a good alibi," I said, egging him on. "You think the cops will buy it?"

Dane reached for his pocket and I jumped a little.

"Relax," he said, pulling out his phone. He clicked around and then showed me the screen. On Dane's phone was his Metro app that showed a timestamp of when he'd jumped on the bus, just moments before the shots.

"They'll buy it all right. I got the proof. I ain't have shit to do with that, and plus . . ." Dane trailed off, catching himself.

"Plus what?" I asked impatiently.

"That lady, Melissa. I'd seen her around before, with Jason. She would be in the basement sometimes when we kicked it. To be honest, I'm pretty sure he was smashing shorty. But recently, she ain't been around. Then all of a sudden, she pops up dead? Him arrested . . ."

Dane was painting a picture I refused to accept. Mo and I had assumed Jason and Donna had some sort of connection, but to know they were actively kicking it was a bombshell.

Dane shifted his weight and looked around again.

"Yo," he said, grabbing my attention. "I already wasted too much time staking this place out. Last thing I'll say is this, if anybody ask, you don't know nothing. Me and you never even met. Stay dangerous."

I couldn't speak. The revelation he'd just dropped on me was heavy enough to freeze me in place. By the time I shook it off, he was halfway to the exit of the park.

"Yo, D!" I called out, stopping him in his tracks. "You heard from Rico?"

"That man disappeared," Dane said, shaking his head. "You should, too, li'l homie."

And with that, he was gone, leaving me with more questions than answers.

This was becoming a theme and I hated it. Dane didn't seem as concerned with figuring out what really happened with Jason as I was. In fact, he seemed pretty convinced he was the shooter.

CHAPTER TWELVE
MONIQUE
SOME GOOD NEWS

What was a cool day turned into a rainy one, then turned into a stormy one, with winds so wrathful that I thought they'd sweep our house away. Lightning ripped through the sky and thunder cracked, scaring me a little. I felt safer when Coop arrived at my door.

Knock, knock, knock . . .

I got up and walked to the front door, quickening my steps to get him out of the rain as quickly as I could. I swung the door open and—

"Hey," he said as I gave him room to hurriedly come in. "It's nasty out there."

"Yeah, weird weather for the middle of summer."

"When is it not weird weather in this city?" he scoffed as he kicked off his shoes.

He picked the same couch he always did, sat down, and wiped a few droplets of water from his face. The raindrops collected like little diamonds in his hair. I almost forgot my manners just looking at him. But I snapped myself out of it and went to get him a towel from the bathroom.

But when I came back in, I stopped in my tracks. His shirt was off. His damp tank top clung to his chest and abs. His shoulders were broad and bronze. Cooper had definitely grown up.

"Here ya go," I said as I handed it to him.

"Thanks," he said. "Mind if I put my shirt in your dryer? I got soaked."

"Of course," I said, taking his shirt.

"Wha—"

"So—"

We tripped over each other's words. The silence right after quickly bubbled into one of those awkward moments between two people with a romantic tension neither want to acknowledge. I smiled at him and he smiled back with those pretty white teeth. I wanted him to make the first move. No way I was.

"You first," I said.

"I was just gonna ask about Jay—how is he?"

"How would you be?" I huffed.

"Point taken."

"One thing I do know is he didn't do it," I said confidently.

"Did you ever doubt him?" Coop asked.

"No!" I hit back fast. Although, I still wasn't sure if that was entirely true and it had been eating me up. "I mean . . . I guess there *was* this little bit of doubt in the back of my mind. But it's gone now."

Coop nodded. I loved that he didn't judge me for thinking my brother could have something to do with such a horrific crime. But I needed to remain objective if I wanted the facts. Too many people were only ever seeing the truth they wanted to see.

"What changed?" Coop asked.

"I was finally able to look into his eyes. I know when he's lying. I would have been able to tell."

Coop started to pick at his lucky bracelet. That was always a telltale sign that something was on his mind.

"What you thinking, Coop?"

"I . . . I did some digging like we talked about, and found out one of the guys who Jay was with the day of the shooting. I think his name was . . . Dwayne?"

"Dwayne . . . you mean Dane?" I said, sitting up.

"Yeah, that's the one," Coop said, standing up and pacing around the room. Something was definitely bothering him.

"Coop, that's great, right?! This could be the break we need. Let's go. We need to talk to him ASAP!"

"Uh, I actually already did, while you went to see Jason. If you were there he wouldn't have talked, I just know it."

"Umm, okay, but you're just now saying something?" I asked in disbelief.

Coop was being weird. It was like he was keeping something from me, but what?

"I mean it just happened, right before I came over."

"Okay, so what he say?"

"Well, he said Jay and Donna did in fact know each other. Pretty well. He was implying . . . you know . . ."

"What are you saying, Coop?" I snapped. "Spit it out already."

"He said they were hooking up," Coop blurted out. "They were dating. He's seen her in your house, Mo. In Jay's basement. Anyway, he showed me a timestamp on his Metro app. He was on a bus when the shots went off. He wasn't with Jay and wouldn't be an alibi for him."

I turned away from him, looking off into the distance. I needed a moment for the words to settle in my brain. I couldn't believe what I was hearing. Here I am pointing out that statistically the most logical suspect is Donna's lover, whoever that may be, and that turns out to be Jason?

"That's impossible. I've never seen her. And I asked Jason if he knew Donna and he said no," I shot back.

Coop thought for a second and slowly turned his head to meet my gaze. "Did you ask him if he knew Donna or Melissa? Her real name hasn't been released."

Vertigo hit me at the weight of Coop's words.

I had asked Jason if he knew *Donna*, not *Melissa*. He hadn't even flinched. Clearly, he knew exactly who I was talking about, even though her name had been revealed as Melissa.

Coop must've seen the shock on my face because he moved in closer and put an arm around me. "It's okay. Maybe there's a reason. Maybe his lawyer told him her real name or something."

I appreciated Coop for trying, but it didn't help much. The intrusive thoughts were already there.

"Coop, do you think the cops know about Jay and Donna's . . . relationship?"

"For our sake, I hope not. It's likely they'll find out though, which doesn't look good for Jay." Coop dropped his face in his hands.

This was getting ugly, and we both might lose our brother forever.

"It's okay, we just have to keep going. Dane say who else was there?" I asked, regaining my faculties. The only thing to do was to move ahead with the investigation.

"He did—Rico. Said Rico was the one who gave Jay the gun. But nobody can find him now. No online activity, either."

More devastating news. Rico had just come home from prison. *What the hell was he doing with a gun?* I tried not to ever judge Jason's friends, but the more Cooper spoke, the more disappointed I became.

"And who's the last person?" I asked finally.

"What do you mean?" Coop replied, looking surprised.

"Well, there were four guys in all the photos released, including Jay. We've only accounted for three."

"Oh, uh, Dane said he didn't know the other guy. Never seen him around."

"Hmm, that's odd. Rico and Dane are some of Jay's closest friends. People he trusts. You'd think they all knew each other."

Coop rubbed his brow and squinted his eyes. All these unsolved questions were getting to him.

"Yeah, you'd think. But who knows, sounds like Jason wasn't thinking straight," Coop said.

And he wasn't wrong. I suddenly understood why Coop was being so weird. Jason was starting to look guilty. Even though Coop and Jason were cool, Jason going to prison wouldn't upset Coop's life the way it would mine. Perhaps Coop wanted nothing more to do with this. It wasn't looking good for my brother.

"I really appreciate you, Coop. And I want you to know if you ever feel like this is too much, you can stop. I know what all this looks and sounds like, but I just don't believe Jason would do this. I'm sorry I even roped you in."

Coop's strong hand rubbed my back.

"Mo, we in this together. I got you. Jason is like my older brother, too, you know that."

I looked into his eyes and could tell he meant every word.

"Thank you, Coop. I couldn't do this without you. Would you mind digging some more? We need to figure out who that last person was."

"For sure, I'm on it," Coop assured me.

"As for Rico," I continued. "He's definitely a suspect, especially if he had the gun first. Until he turns up, we need to follow any other leads. And you're right, there has to be an explanation for why Jason lied," I huffed, standing up and shaking off my brief moment of dejectedness.

"Did Jason say anything else?" Coop asked.

"You know, he did say something kind of weird at the end of our visit. 'Follow the sphinx.' That mean anything to you?"

"Nah, I don't even know what a sphinx is."

"Me neither, something related to Ancient Egypt, I think. Let's look it up."

Coop typed in "sphinx" on the computer and a few different images popped up of huge statues in Egypt, all bearing the head of a pharaoh, the body of a lion, and the wings of an eagle.

"Interesting, reminds me a little of that pamphlet you showed me," I said offhandedly.

Coop's eyes started to bulge. "That's it! Mo, you're a genius."

He jumped up to grab the pamphlet; the creature on the front was very similar. Except its head was a wolf and its wings were more dragon-like than eagle. But there was no mistaking, this was some type of sphinx. "It's not just a coincidence. It's gotta mean something."

"If that's the case," I jumped in, "finding out where this pamphlet came from should lead us somewhere."

"Or to someone."

We both stared at each other as we realized the magnitude of what we found. Finally, some good news.

CHAPTER THIRTEEN
COOPER
RAH

Finally, we had some leads: the sphinx, the phrase "the time is now," and Jay's connection to Donna. I'd never heard Jay mention anything about any of this. I felt like I was with him more than Mo was, but there was so much to him that I had no clue about. So many secrets.

One thing was for sure though: The pressure to find a suspect other than Jason was heating up. I finally understood why Dane said Jason was *cooked*. Whether he did it or not, once the cops connected him to Donna, it was a wrap, he was going down. And I'd likely go down with him.

CLICK.

Mo snapped a picture of the front of her pamphlet.

"What're you gonna do with that?"

"Google image search."

I was glad she was so handy with the internet, because I was not.

"There's a video here," Mo said, perking up. I practically jumped over to her to see what she was talking about. She clicked on a thumbnail, which happened to be the insignia from the pamphlets.

"This is it. We're literally following the sphinx," I said as Mo navigated the page. In some weird way I was getting excited. I kept thinking about the possibility of being on the other side of this, when I wouldn't be facing the threat of prison. It was all that kept me going.

Well, and being with Mo.

Mo clicked on the most recent video, one posted a few days before the protest. It featured a guy dressed in a red, black, and green dashiki.

"Yoooo, Rah here. I need y'all to listen up! What's happening in this city ain't an accident. Black kids getting killed by cops ain't random. First, they killed our men. Then our women, and now our children. People out of work? It ain't *just the times*. There are a lot of people in this city making money, it's just they don't look like me. Probably don't look like you, either. We need to step it up . . ."

Rah tilted his screen up just enough to reveal a rifle hanging on his wall in the background.

". . . We need to take up arms and protect ourselves from the powers that work so hard to keep us oppressed. So if you want to learn how we can start a real revolution, pull up. It's tax season—"

The video abruptly ended.

"Tax season?" I whispered under my breath.

"Hmph. Who the hell *is* this guy?" Mo asked.

"What's the profile name?" I asked.

"Says BLU. Coop, this man looks crazy. Is this what Jason wanted us to see?"

"I mean, it's definitely the same logo as the pamphlets. Scroll down to another video."

Mo clicked Play once again, and we both watched, horrified.

Just weeks ago the man, Rah, had put up a video calling for looting and rioting at the protest for Samir. My stomach sank. Rah had organized the riots.

"Let me see something," I said, reaching out to take the computer.

"He's behind all of this," Mo gasped before steadying her voice. "This is who corrupted my brother."

I scrolled down to the video caption and there was a button that read—

SUBSCRIBE TO RECEIVE UPDATES

I clicked it and typed in the email I'd just made up for my THR1FT account. As soon as I pressed Enter, my phone buzzed with an email from Rah.

"What is it? What are you doing?" Mo asked, jumping up.

"Subscribing, trying to see what else we can learn." I opened my email.

Dear Soldier,

It's time to break the chains of silence. For too long, the truth has been hidden from us, much like the secrets guarded beneath the ancient sphinxes of Egypt. White supremacists have held the truth hostage for far too long, obscuring it with a veil of deception. But today, they don't walk around in hoods and robes brandishing crosses anymore. They wear a uniform of a different kind. They are the men and women in blue brandishing badges and cuffs. They are the puppeteers in the suits down there at your capitol building, twisting and contorting the rules to fit their agenda and destroy ours. It's tax season.

THE TIME IS NOW

TOMORROW—9PM
271 Georgia Ave NW, Washington, DC 20001

Rah Meck

That phrase again, tax season. I realized that I had been following a big brother who himself had been following a YouTube villain. *I've been following a follower.*

"I can't believe Jay was listening to this scumbag!"

"Hey." I put my arm around her. "Maybe Jay was feeling his message, as misguided as it might've been of him," I said, thinking back to how I'd been convinced by Jay to join in these shenanigans in the first place. And I could understand what Rah was saying, even if his delivery was aggressive.

"Cooper, his message is violence. He literally has a rifle hanging on his wall. That's how Jay's in the mess he's in now, for having a gun. He's misleading the people. You can't fight fire with fire," Mo spat. "Did I tell you that one of them looting goons was hiding in the crowd right behind me before the shots went off? A skirmish broke out because of him. For all I know, he could've had a gun and used it on me. My life could've been in danger. It's sickening."

My heart skipped a beat. I felt myself getting defensive. Mo was using words like *goons* and *sickening*, but I wasn't any of those things.

"I'm just saying your perspective isn't the only one," I said, backing off. "And it isn't automatically right just because it's yours," I said, stepping back in it.

"Yeah well, at least I have a perspective on this thing. You weren't even at the protest," Mo shot back.

We sat there quiet for a bit. I could feel the fury coming off her and I wanted nothing more than to calm her down, but I couldn't even keep myself calm. I tried to breathe through it. It seemed to work momentarily, but the truth was this whole ordeal was stressing us both out.

"I'm sorry, Coop. I'm just . . . This is all too much."

Tears started to fall down her face and all I could do was move in and put my arm around her. In that moment, I almost felt like giving up, but I had to stay strong for both of us. I pulled Mo in tighter, putting her head on my chest.

"It's okay, Mo. We're trying to figure out a whole murder. This is stressful. You don't have to feel bad. And I do agree, this guy seems hostile. However, we know he's connected to both Jason and Donna. And the protest! I've said it once, I'll say it again: Can't be a coincidence. I think we should go to this event and dig for clues."

Mo straightened up and wiped her face. Just like that she was back to her hardened self.

"You're right, Coop," Mo said, gazing at me. "Let's do it. Let's go."

CHAPTER FOURTEEN
MONIQUE
BLU

DREAMS

In the concrete jungle where dreams take flight,
I paint a vision of a world, pure and bright.
Where no more the sirens wail, or streets in strife,
Just harmony and peace, the essence of life.

A day when the city's heartbeat sings,
And drowns out the gunshot rings.
Black lives thriving in the summer heat,
And every corner boasting a hopeful beat.

Graffiti on walls tells tales of peace,
Unity and love, the struggles cease.
There's no more tears on a mother's face,
Just pride in her eyes, with a loving embrace.

Let this dream be the calm to the storm,
In the heart of the city, where the stars are born.
A day when every block in every hood finds its grace,
A world where every soul, every spirit finds their place.

I put my phone down as I finished typing the last stanza of my poem. Writing poetry had always been my way of blowing off steam. I just had to get my feelings out of my head onto paper. When I was younger, whenever I'd get mad or sad, my mom would say, "The pen is mightier than the sword, baby girl."

So, I worked to become mighty.

Although, I didn't feel so mighty right now. And I was definitely confused. I'd always liked to think that my brother loved me too much to deceive me. But realizing he flat-out lied to me and Mom about knowing Donna had me shook. Not because it made me question his love, but because it made me question his innocence.

If there was ever a time to use my words, it was now. Things needed to change in this city. No, in this country. Better yet, around the world.

Except this Rah guy was going about it all wrong. Setting us back even. What was the point of stooping to the level of the oppressor? What was the point of giving them the ammunition to say that we deserve to be shot in the streets? You could never convince me that this was the way to have our voices heard. Especially now after that line of thinking had gotten my brother arrested.

In any case, Rah was our only real lead. He had means, access, and now we just needed to find a motive.

I looked out the window and the sky was blacker than usual. A bad omen.

"Come on, Coop, come on," I whispered to myself.

We had planned to take Jason's car to see Rah. My mom wouldn't miss it. Cooper just had to get to my house before my mom got home. She'd ask a million questions and probably wouldn't even let me leave. But I figured I'd ask for forgiveness instead of permission.

Suddenly I heard my mom at the door.

"Yeah, she's here I'm sure," I heard my mom say to someone. And I knew exactly who that someone was.

By the time I reached the top of the stairs, Coop was already sitting on the couch with my mom talking his ear off.

"Oh, there you are. Look who I found," my mom said with a mischievous grin. She had always been amused by my and Coop's relationship. As kids she would even make jokes about us going to prom or off to college together. She had no qualms about embarrassing me.

"Yes, Ma, I could hear you all the way upstairs. Hey, Coop."

"Hey," he replied shyly.

"So . . . Coop was saying y'all may be going somewhere. That was a surprise to me."

"Yeah, about that. Something just came up."

"Something like? It's late and you know folks are tripping out there."

"It's a rally," Coop stepped in. "For Samir."

"At the last rally, a murder occurred and my son ended up arrested."

"This one will be different, Mom," I said, backing Coop up. "Much more private, secure."

I could see my mom considering.

"Ma, I really need to get out of this house," I said, laying it on. "I can't think anymore sitting in that room."

My mom twisted her face and looked at Cooper.

"Cooper, you going to take care of my little girl?"

"Yes, ma'am."

"Um, excuse me, let's not act like I can't take care of myself. Come on, Ma."

"Uh-huh. Fine, but be back by a decent hour, you understand?" my mom said, heading to the kitchen.

"Yes, ma'am," Coop and I shouted in unison, heading out the door before my mom had a chance to change her mind.

Outside the air felt perfect. The stars were shining brighter than I'd seen them in a while. The night felt almost romantic in a way as Cooper and I headed to Jason's car. Wasn't the first date I had imagined, but I had butterflies just the same.

I wondered if Coop was still a little upset about the shot I threw at him about not attending the protest.

"Hey, I really am sorry about what I said yesterday. I just lost it."

Coop shook his head. "Oh that? Forget about it, for real. We good."

"Okay cool. You just seem quiet."

"Just trying to imagine what we're walking into, you know?"

"I do know."

We kept walking in silence and pretty soon we were at Jason's car.

Hopping inside was like being transported to another time. A time when Jason had been here. When he'd been a straight-A student in middle school and the star quarterback in Pop Warner. The car smelled just like him. I even had to toss an old jacket of his to the back seat.

Coop drove off and the streetlights flashed by like a neon puzzle and the sounds of city traffic drowned out my negative thoughts.

I looked out the window and saw we weren't far from the venue.

"Don't be scared, I got you," Coop said, taking my hand. His touch sent shock waves through my body.

"I know," I said, looking over at him and locking eyes for a split second.

He put his eyes back on the road, but I couldn't turn away. Maybe because I felt safe with him. Maybe it was the way his strong fingers wrapped around mine. Maybe it was all of the above. But everything about the moment felt right, except for the fact we were trying to solve a murder of course.

Coop slowed to park the car and we looked around to get our bearings. The building was on the seedier side of town, but not too far down the beaten track that I would have hesitated to go alone had Coop not been here. Still, this wasn't the most inviting of affairs.

"Aight, let's do it," Coop said, hopping out. As I stepped out and around the car, I wrapped my arm around his and huddled close.

As we walked up a series of stairs to the building, we could hear the energy pour out through the doors. A few people ahead of us were being let in by a large burly man at the door.

A sudden rush of doubt hit me. What were we doing? What if this Rah person was actually a murderer? We were in no position to confront him. We had no master plan, just blind curiosity and a need to solve this case. I wanted to run, but I felt myself take a step forward with Coop.

"Name?" the man asked.

"Should be Conor."

The man checked his clipboard and darted his eyes back to Coop. "And who is this?"

"She's my plus-one," Coop said.

"We need your name and email," the man said, handing me his clipboard and pen.

I wrote in a random name and email and handed it back to the man.

"Come on," he said, letting us in.

I froze for a minute. I had half been expecting that we wouldn't make it past this point. Or maybe that was just something I was secretly hoping deep down.

Inside, the place was buzzing with energy. My eyes scanned the room for Rah but everybody looked the same. Men and women all wore similar garb, dashikis or clothes with African print. And, much to my surprise, everyone was so young, our age or just a few years older.

"There he is," Coop said, reading my mind.

Rah Meck emerged from a back room and was clearly the man of the hour, and he knew it. The look on his face was a mixture of pure confidence and a hint of soullessness that only glinted when he thought nobody else was looking. But I was looking. And so was Coop.

Rah was a little taller in person, but also looked younger. He must've been about twenty-five.

"Ayo, you gotta move," a voice growled from behind us. It was Big Man from the front door. I hadn't even realized that we were taking up space in the entrance, standing in a trance as we watched the man who could very well be responsible for the nightmare wreaking havoc on our lives.

I turned to see a tall man in a custom suit standing inside the door. He was sizing us up and I did the same, taking in the sight of the sphinx ring on his index finger and the bloodred tie peeping out the top of his jacket.

"Let's get settled," I whispered, grabbing Coop's hand and leading him toward a seat just a few rows back from the front. I made sure to pick two seats off to the side. It seemed like the safest vantage point in case anything popped off.

As we got closer to the front of the room, the reason why people gravitated toward Rah became clear. There was a charisma about him and an appeal that was undeniable. He was like a force unto himself, holding the crowd in the palm of his hand. The air hummed with the electric energy of the city as he prepared to address the crowd.

"I want to thank each and every one of you for coming out tonight. Right now, there is something serious that we need to discuss as a community. The powers that be in this town," his voice boomed as he paced around, carefully choosing his words, "want to erase us, but we won't let 'em. They know good and well, the future of the Black American depends on its youth. Which is why they underfund your schools. They cut your summer jobs. They give you access to guns and they flood your neighborhoods with drugs."

"FACTS!" a kid yelled from the back of the room.

"That's why I'm proposing a new type of organization. Not

a Black Panther *Party*, not a MOVE *movement*, not an *association* like our NAACP. No. Today I propose a new kind of organization. One that this country can't destroy. A *union*. This country has profited off our backs for long enough. It's time we came together as one collective voice, and that starts right here. Right here in DC, Chocolate City, with the young people of the nation's capital. Now it's your time. History will look back at the moment the Black Labor Union was born and declare it the most pivotal movement in human history. Let's take this city back, then the country!"

The crowd echoed Rah's call to action. To them, he was the man with the plan, and he was going to be the savior who uplifted this community, which had been pushed to the brink.

"Trust me, they are scared of us. I know because they are watching us. In this very room, we had an undercover fed watching our every move."

"What the hell?" I whispered to Coop. But he looked to be in more shock than I was. "He has to be talking about Donna!"

"I'll keep saying it—it ain't a coincidence. Follow the sphinx," he whispered back.

All of a sudden, we had the missing piece. Motive. If Rah had found out Donna was attending these so-called meetings with the intention to bring his movement down, I'm sure he would've been furious. I started to feel like I was looking at our new suspect.

We sat there listening to Rah speak, enrapturing the crowd with his promises and smooth speech. When he was done, a fervor had overtaken the room. He made an announcement, calling all new potential members to the front to officially join the BLU.

It was like BLU's very own altar call, as if they were going to baptize us in the blood of Rah.

"This is the perfect excuse to get some one-on-one time with Rah and find out what he knows," I said.

"But what's the plan? I don't know if we necessarily want one-on-one time with this guy," Coop whispered back.

Coop reminded me of something. If Rah was willing to kill a cop for messing with his plans, what would he do to us if he knew our real intention?

I looked around at the crowded room. This was as good a time as any to see what we could learn. Rah was too smart to try anything with all his followers present.

"No way he does anything here. Guys like this are narcissists. Just get him talking about his vision, BLU, give him lots of compliments, and as he loosens up we'll hit him with the tough questions to see what we can learn."

"Sounds good to me, let's do it."

One by one, people trickled into an office just behind the stage where Rah had gone after finishing his speech. Before long, Coop and I were up.

"Right this way," the bouncer from earlier called out. As we followed him to the back, Coop nudged me, calling attention to a weapon protruding from under his shirt. I knew what it was.

Just as we got to the door, Rah opened it.

"Appreciate it, Rock," Rah said as he sized up Coop and me. "Right this way, youngins." We walked in and Rock closed the door behind us.

We were in the lion's den now.

Inside, Rah's office was messier than I imagined. The unmistakable scent of old books and brewing coffee filled the air. My eyes were immediately drawn to the well-worn desk, its surface covered in papers peppered with notes and scribbles, interspersed with books like *The Autobiography of Malcolm X*, *The Art of War*, and *The 48 Laws of Power*.

The walls were a canvas of inspirational posters and artwork that screamed resistance and hope. Images of iconic revolutionaries gazed down at me, some of whom even I didn't recognize. One for sure I knew was Fred Hampton, his silent stare igniting a fire in my chest.

On top of an antique floor safe were pictures of Rah with other local activists, politicians, and thought leaders. Rah smiled in not one photo, his eyes serious and commanding.

For a moment I felt inspired, and I started to understand why Jason was following this man. He was *inspiring*. Like so many of us in the city, we were looking for something to ignite us, to point us in the right direction because nowadays everything seems so confusing. We had no leaders. But even though I understood, I remembered that this man was possibly tied to my big brother being arrested for murder. And we were here to find out how.

"Conor, huh," Rah quipped as we sat down in front of him. "And who is this?" he said, looking at me.

Cooper sat down beside me as the folding chair squeaked beneath his weight.

"Zo," I said calmly.

"Hmm. I've never seen y'all around," Rah said, standing up and walking to the back of the room. "How'd you hear about us?"

His voice was deep and smooth, but my heart was pounding in my ears as I imagined what he might be going to retrieve. But thankfully he just went to pour himself a drink.

"Found this on the bus," Coop said as he put one of the pamphlets we found on the desk. "We looked you up and wanted to learn more. What exactly is a union?"

Rah looked down at the pamphlet and smirked at his own handiwork. He took a seat facing us.

"A union is a lot like the mob. It's a group of people that want the same thing. Its power is not only in numbers, but the fact that there is unity. Solidarity. The body follows the head."

"What if the head is corrupt?" I asked.

"There's checks and balances," Rah replied, glaring at me.

"Sounds genius. So what do you offer?" Coop said, jumping in.

"We offer all the things this country promises but fails to deliver. Food, shelter, medical. Everything one needs to survive. Through this, we can build our own nation within a nation."

I looked at Coop, who seemed to be eating up every word that Rah said. It was making me sick. Even though he talked a good game, I knew this guy had an angle.

"Yes, that does sound powerful, but how do you plan to provide all of that?" I asked.

"Well there are dues members have to pay."

And there it was.

"So you're charging people to be in your fight for empowerment?"

Rah sat back in his chair.

"Is there something you'd like to say, young lady?"

"I've said it."

Coop kicked my leg underneath our chairs. I knew the plan, but Rah's smug face bothered me. The air got thick and I could feel the tension between us.

"Well, uh, you're doing great work, Rah," Coop said, once again trying to stick to the plan. I was glad he did. I'd almost let my disdain for Rah blow this whole thing. "You must be doing something right. We heard you mention being under surveillance. That's crazy."

"Yeah," Rah muttered, twirling his cup of whiskey.

"What happened to the snitch?" I asked, desperately trying to change my approach.

Rah leaned back in his chair. "You know, I think it's time y'all left. You ask the wrong questions, you say the wrong things," Rah said, standing up.

I started to panic. We couldn't lose him because we'd never get behind these walls again. I had to act fast. Rah reached for the door when—

"Was it Donna?" I blurted out. The instant I said it I regretted it.

"Excuse me?" Rah said, slow and deliberate.

But I didn't repeat it. Instead, I bolted to my feet, Coop right on my heels. I started looking around the room for anything I could use as a weapon if this turned ugly.

Rah was frozen still, like he'd seen a ghost. Until finally, instead of opening the door, he locked it.

CHAPTER FIFTEEN
COOPER
REVELATIONS

"What the hell are you thinking?" I tried to telepathically yell at Mo. She had just blown our cover.

"Sit down," Rah said quietly.

Neither of us could move, our feet were bolted to the floor.

"I said SIT DOWN!"

So we did.

He came over and sat back down, huffing and puffing along the way.

"What do you know about Donna?" Rah snarled at Mo.

"We know everything!" I said, jumping in. Of course we didn't, but I wanted to shoot the energy he was giving Mo right back at him.

Rah looked at me and leaned back in his chair. "Really? Then tell me who killed her," he said, calling my bluff.

We were stumped. I wasn't sure if it was smart to flat-out accuse him. If we were right, I didn't see why he'd be eager to let us go.

"Look, we'll cut to the chase," Mo said. "My real name is Monique, Monique Simms. I'm Jason Simms's little sister."

"*You're* Jason's sister?"

"Yes. And as you may know he's being accused of this murder and I don't think he did it. Neither of us do," Mo said, her voice cracking. "Now we're here to figure out what happened to Donna and we think you may know more than you're letting on."

"Yeah, especially considering that speech you just gave," I chimed in as I placed a hand on Mo's knee to keep her calm. "We know she's been here, you just admitted it. So you had access. You organized the riots, so you had opportunity. And you finding out she was an agent gives you motive. So tell us what really happened!"

Rah's face turned from anger to amusement as he rubbed his hand across his face. He leaned back in his chair and let out one of the creepiest laughs I ever heard. It wasn't so much the laugh that was creepy, but the fact he was laughing as a response to being accused of murder.

Then he stopped and sat quietly. I could hear Mo's watch ticking away as Rah exhaled slowly.

"I appreciate the gumption, I do, but you have no idea what you've stepped into, do you?" he finally said.

"What do you mean?" Mo asked.

"I mean you two think you got it all figured out and couldn't be further from the truth. Donna wasn't just a government agent. She was our deep mole. A double agent if you will," he said.

I scratched the back of my head. "Huh?!"

"Look," Rah said as he turned his focus back to Mo. "Donna worked for the cause. I mean, not at first. She had infiltrated, through Jay actually. I'm not sure if they were an item or what. And she would've been successful right here under our noses. Except about a month ago she came to me and not only confessed to being an agent, but said she had info I may be interested in."

"Samir," I whispered to myself.

"Smart, young brother. Exactly. She told me she had info on the shooting that turned her stomach. Made her realize she was literally working for the bad guy. These docs and classified files would've given BLU the power we needed."

"What kind of power?" Mo asked.

"Political leverage. Dirt on the powers that be. A bargaining tool."

"You mean extortion?" Mo shot back.

"All these people understand is the strong arm."

"The pen is mightier than the sword."

Rah smirked. "And who gave us that line? The same white man that doesn't want you to pick up that sword."

It was the first time I had seen Mo silenced.

"Have you all heard of Andrew McDonald?" Rah continued.

Mo and I shook our heads.

"Well, he was a cop back in the day. His partner killed a kid in a very similar fashion to Samir, at a metro station."

"Oh yes, Davon Marcus," Mo said, finding her voice again. "I know that case well. We were kids when it happened but it always stuck with me. I've been thinking about Davon ever since Samir was killed. I even mentioned him in my speech at the protest. I don't remember an Andrew McDonald, though."

"Yeah, that's because he was erased. Cut from the story. After

Davon died, Andrew threw away his uniform and replaced it with a revolutionary's. He planted the first seeds of the BLU way back then. You see, this isn't new. But Donna was trying to help us find a new way to fight."

Our worlds were upended. Could Rah and Donna really have been working together like he claimed? But the way he talked about her during his speech didn't match that energy.

"You claim you were working with Donna, but out there," I said, pointing to the main room, "it seemed like you hated her. Like she was a *threat*."

"It's called selling it. Recently, Donna felt like she was being followed. She didn't want to come here anymore. Hell, I didn't want her here either if it meant it could expose our whole operation. So, in case they've sent another operative in, I don't want them to catch on that her and I were working together. Because if so, whoever killed Donna would be coming after me next."

"How does Jason fit in to all this?" I asked.

Rah took a long pause. Longer than I would've liked.

"You know, I will say, Donna and Jason's relationship didn't seem necessarily platonic, if you know what I mean."

Mo and I looked at each other. It was the same thing Dane had alluded to.

"But if I had to guess," Rah continued, "I don't see the young brother pulling the trigger."

"Who do you think did?" Mo asked.

"Tell me, in your . . . findings, did you learn who Melissa's partner was? Ex-partner?"

He took our silence as an opportunity to continue.

"David Peters."

He said the name like it was supposed to mean something to me, but I was drawing a blank. I looked over to Mo and I could tell something was rattling in her head.

"The cop who killed Samir."

"Y'all are sharp, I'll give you that. If I had to bet, that's the guy. Not only did he shoot Samir, but he's caught up in some shady secret society. Donna found the evidence. And whatever it was, they definitely didn't want it to be released. So I believe he was tasked with putting an end to that threat."

The words sunk in like ice in my veins. To think another cop had committed murder right on the heels of Samir's death was horrifying. And he'd killed his own partner?!

"In any case," Rah continued, "Donna was supposed to hand off the incriminating documents during the protest while things were in chaos, just in case she was being followed."

"That's why you planned the riots?" Mo asked.

"Yes. A distraction. This is warfare. But also, because I believe we deserve to unleash our rage. We are angry, and rightfully so."

Rah turned away as his voice started to crack. "But Donna never showed up to our meeting spot. And when the news broke about the body, I didn't need them to tell me who it was. I knew."

Mo and I exchanged a knowing glance. I knew what she was thinking because I was thinking it, too. Perhaps we were too quick to judge Rah.

We sat quiet for a second, stunned by this revelation. I almost wanted to comfort this man who'd seemed like such a powerful force just a few moments ago.

Rah pulled himself together as he turned back toward us, taking a deep breath.

"By the way," Rah said, turning to Mo, "your brother is a sharp young man, dedicated to the cause. I'm sorry for what you and your family are going through. I wish I could be of more support, but you must understand I need to distance myself from this situation. I am working toward something greater."

Mo nodded, but I could still see the wariness plain on her face.

"Thank you," she said.

Rah stuck out his hand and Mo shook it. Then he turned to me and I shook it as well.

"Yeah, thank you. And sorry for coming in so hot."

"No need to apologize, young brother. I would do the same for the people I love. Now look, I do have somewhere to be. You two put your names and numbers down and we'll keep each other in the loop, what do you say?" Rah said, extending a pen.

"Sounds good," I replied, grabbing the pen and jotting my name and cell number. I extended the pen to Mo.

"I'm good," she said, staring Rah down, clearly unsure if she should trust him or not.

I understood, even though I didn't feel the same apprehension I'd felt when we first entered the building. Rah smiled and held up his hand, dismissing us.

"Yo, one more thing," Rah called out as we headed to the door, stopping us in our tracks.

"Donna mentioned a rat. A confidential informant code-named Viper that was in our midst as well. I never figured out who it was, but could be tied to Jason."

"The anonymous tip that led the cops straight to Jay?" I said, looking at Mo.

She nodded in agreement.

WOOWOOWOOWOOWOOWOO!

A cop car sped past as we stepped out onto the sidewalk.

"Dirty cops, double agents, confidential informants, what in the world have we gotten ourselves into, Coop?" Mo asked.

I was asking myself the same thing. My stomach turned knowing I'd been with Jason the day of the murder. Things were getting more and more complicated by the second and much like Mo, I wasn't sure what I had gotten involved in.

But I was deeply involved. Mo was a bystander by comparison. Things could only get worse for me. And here I was hiding the truth, lying through my teeth to the one person I wanted to tell most in the world.

"I don't know, but Rah doesn't seem to be the man we thought he was. Looks like there's a method to the madness."

"Yeah, but looks can be deceiving. We'll keep a watchful eye." Mo leaned over and put her head on my shoulder. "I'm tired, Coop."

I threw my arm around her and held her close. Her warmth against mine felt good. I tried to ignore the guilt stewing in my stomach.

"I know, me too. But we're going to figure this out. I promise."

It was a promise I desperately hoped I could keep. My mind

was spinning at this point. There was so much that we didn't actually know about Donna, about the city we were living in, about the cops we were supposed to be protected by—maybe even about Jay.

"I think we're really getting somewhere," I continued. "We have a new suspect, this David Peters. He also had means, access, and motive. Very, very strong motive. And if Jason and Donna really were seeing each other, or spending time together, I'm sure David figured he'd be the perfect fall guy."

"You're right," Mo said as I opened the car door for her. "So now we need to find the cop who killed Samir. We find David Peters."

CHAPTER SIXTEEN

MONIQUE
FEAR

FEAR

F *is for our FIGHT, our Freedom, our Faith,*
Fierce, as we march forward each day . . .

E *is for EQUITY, which we strive to achieve,*
Waiting for the dream dreamt by Dr. Martin Luther King . . .

A *is for an AWAKENING we all can feel,*
It's fueled by the blood that our ancestors spilled . . .

R *is for REVOLUTION, our mission, our song,*
A resounding resolution to undo this great wrong . . .

So hear our cry and feel the beat of our heart,
from the chains of FEAR, we have chosen to part . . .

Together we stand, united we cheer,
transforming the world, as we conquer . . . our FEAR.

I put down the poem I'd written right after the news of Samir broke. I'd told myself I refused to be afraid of a world that hated me because of the color of my skin. I desperately needed that courage now because just the idea of confronting Officer David Peters terrified me.

I needed to know why he wanted to frame my brother of all people, if he did in fact kill Donna. Though I had an idea. If I had to put this whole thing together, I guessed David had killed Samir and the police covered it up, but Donna knew information about it that would find him guilty. The city, or at least a portion of the police, justice, and/or political force, covered it up and Donna didn't appreciate that. Then David or some arm of the law made sure she was taken care of before she could bring the evidence to light with Rah's help. She was seeing Jason so he was an easy fall guy. It made perfect sense. And usually in these things, the answer that made sense was the right one.

I racked my brain on how I could possibly find a location for this cop. I tried to search property records like we did for Melissa/Donna, but that came up empty.

"*Figures*," I muttered to myself. I'm sure he went off the grid after the shooting. Would've been too easy. So I did what I'm good at and continued to scour the web.

Articles, think pieces, social media rants, there was plenty of information out there about the killing of Samir. Everybody seemed to be on the same page. Samir posed no threat to anyone. He was fleeing the metro station when David Peters opened fire in a public space and killed a fourteen-year-old boy. Even though they apparently found a weapon on Samir. After everything I'd found out, I wondered if Samir had actually been unarmed and that was one of the things Donna was going to bring to light.

I almost buckled at the thought of such a crooked system. The pain was overwhelming so I tried not to think about it.

It was a horrible set of truths to relive, but any clue into Peters's life could've been helpful. That's when I saw one article mention Peters was receiving death threats at work.

"Yes!" I exclaimed out loud. Not because the man was receiving death threats; I didn't believe in an eye for an eye as that would leave us all blind. But the fact that he was receiving threats meant I could probably find his address somewhere, or at least what police precinct he worked out of.

So my search began. The glow of the screen was the only light in my room, casting long shadows that seemed to stretch and twist with every click. The internet's underbelly wasn't a place I ever thought I'd dive into, but here I was, swimming through pages of conspiracy theories and anonymous avatars, all because of a name. A name tied to a badge, and a badge tied to a bullet that had changed everything.

Each forum was like peeling back a layer of the world I desperately tried to avoid on the internet. Flat Earthers, Illuminati exposers, I even came across one of Rah's videos where he talks about the killing of Black kids as an intentional act, part of a larger scheme.

A few weeks ago, I would've said the thought seemed far-fetched, but after this whole ordeal, I could feel my mind changing.

Growing, really. Maybe there were plots against us that were more nefarious than I initially gave the system credit for. Maybe Rah had a point and non-violence wasn't always the *best* solution.

Focus, I reminded myself. *This is the trouble of YouTube rabbit holes.*

The thought was a seed, and it germinated as I delved deeper. I wasn't just a spectator anymore; I was part of my own conspiracy now, seeking an address that wasn't meant to be found. A piece of the puzzle that could either solve everything or blow it all to pieces.

I rubbed my eyes as the night went on, nearly giving up, when finally, there it was. A string of numbers and letters that meant nothing to anyone else but screamed at me from the screen. David's work address.

My breath caught; my fingers hovered over the keyboard. This was it. The point of no return.

> MO: Coop, I know where he is.

> COOP: I'll be there in two . . .

What felt like a split second later, the knock at the door startled me. I jumped out of bed and went to open the door to see Cooper standing there with a goofy smile.

"Dang, you stalking me? You got here quick." I opened the door to let Cooper in.

"Pshh, don't flatter yourself." Coop gave me a playful shove. An excuse to touch me.

"So what you find?"

"Look. It's the address of the police station he works at."

Coop peered down at the computer, but his expression turned sour.

"What's the matter? This is great!" I said.

"This ain't like going to Donna's house, Mo. You want to show up at a police station? And confront a dirty cop about a murder? I mean whether this guy murdered Donna or not, we know he killed Samir. This is really, really dangerous."

Despite Coop's words, and even though I knew how dangerous Officer Peters was, I was very prepared to confront him. Maybe I *had* found some courage through writing.

"Well, what do you suggest?"

"For one, we shouldn't confront him at the station. We need to do it somewhere public so he doesn't haul off and you know . . . end us."

"Good point. So maybe we tail him? See where he leads us and wait for our moment?"

"Still sounds nuts but better than the other option. So then what? We tell him everything we know. That Donna had evidence that could put him and maybe other officers away. Record his response and hope he confesses?"

"Nah, I feel like he's too smart for a confession. And like you said, we don't want to antagonize him. I think we almost want the opposite. We want an alibi."

"An alibi? How'd that help us?"

"If he's our guy, he'll probably make up an alibi that won't hold up. We can shift our focus to proving he lied and bam, we've got him."

"Hmm, smart, Mo. Now you're thinking like a cop!" Coop teased.

He wasn't wrong. Lately I had been watching every cop interrogation on the internet I could find to get better at this whole thing. Confronting a murderous cop meant we had to bring our A game.

We needed to be prepared to take our investigation to the next level.

CHAPTER SEVENTEEN
MONIQUE
KILLER COP

Outside the police station was near silent. The white and red cars parked all around made me feel small and vulnerable, like we were surrounded by a pack of wild dogs. I looked over to Coop and he was slumped down in his seat, almost trying to hide. So I imagined he felt exactly like I did.

"You okay?" I asked.

"Yeah, just trying not to be seen."

"We haven't done anything wrong. I think it's okay."

"Yeah, better safe than sorry, though." Coop breathed heavily.

I guess I understood that.

We parked a safe distance away, our eyes fixed on the stately brick building that undoubtedly held more secrets than its appearance suggested.

Each minute stretched longer than the last as both uniformed and what look liked plainclothes cops exited the building. Finally Cooper grabbed the aux cord and put on some R&B playlist.

"This the best you could find?" I joked, my voice barely above a whisper.

"Just setting the mood," he teased back.

"Yeah, just the mood I like, patiently waiting to confront a killer cop."

We both offered a muffled laugh until the car fell back into silence. But the silence was different this time, charged with an unspoken question about what comes after—after we find the truth, after this adventure ends. Do we just go back to being Monique and Cooper, two friends with an unspoken tension between them?

"I've always admired that about you, Mo," Cooper said suddenly, turning to look at me. His eyes were earnest in the dim light. "You're brave."

My heart skipped a beat. "And you're . . . not so bad," I said with a smirk. "No, but seriously, I appreciate you being you. Always . . . solid."

Coop smiled, a soft, genuine smile that made my stomach do flips. "Guess we make a pretty good team, huh?"

Before I could respond, the front door of the police station opened and out came the man himself. David Peters. The moment felt suspended in time, our earlier conversation hanging in the air like a distant promise. Neither of us are sure of our next move.

Peters said his goodbyes to a couple other officers and headed straight for his car.

"This is it," Cooper whispered, starting the car as Peters drove off. Cooper pulled off, falling in line a safe distance behind.

The earlier uncertainty transformed into a focused determination. We were no longer just Monique and Cooper, awkwardly flirting in the face of danger. We were partners on a mission, bound by a shared goal and maybe, just maybe, something more.

I started to grow increasingly worried about what would happen when we finally confronted the dirty cop, but with Cooper's hand occasionally brushing mine as he shifted gears, I felt a strange sense of courage.

Peters's car slowed as he pulled into a grocery store parking lot.

"Doesn't get much more public than this," Coop said, breaking the silence. "Just gotta figure out how to approach this."

I studied the cop's car and found our way in.

"I got it; follow my lead."

We parked far enough away to not be seen, but still close enough to keep our eyes on Peters. When he got out, we did, too.

The fluorescent lights of the grocery store cast a sterile glow over the aisles, too bright for the late hour. Coop and I moved like shadows, trailing David Peters through the maze of shelves stocked with cans and boxes. I walked softly to keep my sneakers from squeaking against the freshly mopped floor.

There was a darkness over Peters that made him seem out of place among the colorful displays of food and discount signs. I felt like I knew the man after staring at his expressionless face in news segments and headlines.

"Okay, what's the plan, Mo?" Cooper murmured, keeping his eyes on Peters, who was now inspecting a can of coffee.

"Just give me a second," I replied, my voice low.

I did have a plan, but the fear had returned. He was a monster in my eyes. A boogeyman.

But for the love of my brother, I decided to confront that fear.

Peters placed the can back on the shelf and moved on, oblivious to our presence. I felt a surge of adrenaline. It was now or never. I took a deep breath as I stepped closer, Cooper right behind. I prepared myself to speak when—

"Can I help you kids?" Peters asked, spinning to catch us mid-stride. His voice carried a hint of annoyance.

I was stuck.

"Think I didn't notice you following me around the store?" he asked, almost begging us to speak up.

"I uh, I uh . . ." It was like I'd forgotten how to speak. I'd had a plan, but the glare from Peters was too much to bear. I was staring in the face of a man who had killed one of us already and likely framed my brother for Donna's murder. I stood frozen.

Then I felt something tug at my hand, and looked down to see Coop's fingers wrap around mine. It was all I needed.

"I wanted to thank you for your service," I finally got out. I could feel Coop's head snap toward me.

"What?" Peters asked, confused.

"I happened to notice your FOP sticker on your car. We didn't park far from you."

"Hmph. Thanks," Peters muttered before turning to walk away.

Cooper squeezed my hand and I gave him a look that said *trust me*. I needed to disarm Peters. And he was a man, so stroking his ego wouldn't be a bad idea, either. I picked up my pace behind him.

"Yeah, what you all do is so brave," I continued. "And how

you handled those rioters! I don't live far from H Street; I heard about what happened down at the protest."

"Look, I appreciate it, but I'm not here to talk," Peters said, pulling up short. "I just want to get my things and leave, if that's all right with you?"

"Oh yes, of course. Although I was curious, have they heard anything else about the lady who was killed? Morgan?"

"Her name was Melissa!" Peters snapped.

A few customers in the store looked our way, reminding Peters that we weren't alone. Peters took a moment to collect himself as he stared at us.

"Look, I know nothing about that case." Peters glanced down, fidgeting with his hand. Something about the mention of Donna made him uneasy, I just wasn't sure why yet. And for the first time I saw something human beneath the menacing cop exterior. "In fact, I wasn't even at the protest. I was behind a desk down at the precinct. I've been taken off the street and I do admin now," he finally said, the words forced out as if they pained him. "Now please, I'm begging you. Leave me be," Peters said through a clenched jaw as he turned away.

Cooper and I watched him go, the tension slowly ebbing away, leaving behind a mix of triumph and uncertainty. We had safely gotten some sort of an answer from him, which was a success. But there was still work to do.

A hand on my shoulder brought me back to the moment.

"Mo, that was quick thinking. You see how he reacted to the mention of Melissa?"

"I did. It means something, just not sure what."

"Well like you said, at least we have a piece of info to go off. We can verify if he was really on a desk the day of the protest. If he's lying, we press further."

"I agree. But in the meantime, there's one other thread of this thing we still need to track down."

"What's that?"

"Rico."

CHAPTER EIGHTEEN
MONIQUE
DUTY CALLS

I rapped on Coop's door as quickly as I could, trying my best not to bang it down.

"Mo," he greeted me with a beautiful smile as I took him in. His strong hands reached out and pulled me past the threshold, and I walked through a wall of warmth in the entryway before he shut the door behind me.

It wasn't the first time that Coop had pulled me out of the cold. The weather that morning reminded me of the day we laid his mother to rest and I was overcome with emotion. I don't know if it was because I had hardly slept or the pounding migraine that kept coming and going like a wave through my forehead.

"You okay?" Coop asked, sensing my sadness.

"I'm good. Just a headache." I waved it off, turning for the living room and quickly dabbing my eyes.

"You sure?" he asked.

"Yeah," I called back, walking through the living room and toward the kitchen before changing the subject. "Where's your dad?"

"He had to work. Anyway, it gives us space to talk through what we found out last night."

"Yeah." I sighed, coming back to the living room.

I was silent as the migraine moved to the back of my skull.

"Mo?" he asked, noticing that I wasn't responding. "Are you really sure you're good?"

"Yeah, it's just . . . my head," I said, rubbing the back of my neck. "I'll be fine. Let's make the first call."

I put the phone on speaker and dialed the number for the fifth district police station, the digits feeling heavier with each press. The line rang three times before a crisp voice answered, "Fifth district, Officer Martinez speaking."

I froze. I hated talking to cops. We knew we couldn't just come out and ask if David Peters's alibi was the truth, but we had to verify it somehow.

"Hello?" the officer repeated.

"Oh yes, hi, um, I need a bit of help," I started, my voice steady despite the whirlwind of doubt spinning in my head. Cooper leaned forward, watching me with a furrowed brow.

"Just like we planned," he whispered, offering me a bit of confidence.

"A couple weeks back, May second I believe, I spoke with someone at the station around this time, about a case. I had an update I wanted to give him but I can't remember his name. I was hoping you could help me?"

I grit my teeth as the line went silent. It was a long shot, but we needed the officer to give us information that would either confirm Peters was in the office at that day and time, or make us delve deeper into his actual whereabouts when the murder went down.

"Let's see . . . ," the officer finally said, as if looking back through records. "Do you remember anything? Badge number, initials? What the name started with?"

I muted the line. "What should I say?"

"Maybe give him the first initial? White male?"

I unmuted the phone.

"He was definitely a white male. I think his last name started with a *P*?" I said, throwing my hands up.

There was another pause on the other end.

I had a creeping sensation that our ploy was about to blow up in our faces.

Then finally—

"Oh, you must've spoken with Officer Peters. He was on the desk that day. He should be here now; I'll go get him."

My heart sank a little—relief, mixed with an unexpected disappointment. Cooper reached over and hung up the line and we both sat in silence for a moment.

"So, Peters was telling the truth," he said, more to himself than to me.

"Yeah, seems like it," I replied, tapping my finger on the table. But there was a part of me that couldn't shake off the nagging feeling that things were just a bit too convenient. For now though, we had to take it at face value.

"You ready for the next one?" Coop asked, pulling me from my train of thought.

"Sure," I said. But really, I was emotionally drained. Jay had been given the go-ahead to accept phone calls and it couldn't have come at a more fortuitous time because we needed answers. Truthful ones.

The call to the DC Department of Corrections for rerouting to Jay's sector was painstaking. Having to identify as "Monique Simms—sister to an alleged murderer" on a recorded phone call wasn't the way I saw my summer going at all. I breathed through it though and there was a moment of reprieve as the call was patched through. I put my phone on speaker again.

Machine: You are connected..
Jay: Hello?
Me: Hey, Jay, it's me, how are you?
Jay: As good as can be. You? Mom?
Me: We're good. Coop's here.
Coop: Jay, what's good?

Jay went silent. I paused, waiting for him to say something.

Me: You there?
Jay: Yeah, I'm here. Wassup, Coop?

Coop looked at me before leaning in to speak.

Coop: What's good, big bro, how you holding up?
Jay: I'm holding. Not much more I can do from in here.
Coop: I hear you.
Jay: You heard from anybody else?

Anybody else? I thought, looking over at Coop, who looked just as confused as I probably did.

Coop: Huh? Uhm—nah? Nah—no one.
Me: Jay, we don't have much time. We need to talk to you about something.
Jay: Go ahead.
Me: We were at one of Rah Meck's rallies the other night and—
Jay: You were WHERE?

I looked at Coop, wondering if I'd said too much.

Me: It's fine, we're fine. All of that noise later.
Jay: Mo, you can't be hanging around with Meck.

I couldn't help but wonder if Jay was tripping because he thought I'd been somewhere unsafe? Or was he worried about the information we received?

Machine: You have five minutes remaining.
Me: Okay, Jay, but it was really helpful . . . And one of the things he mentioned was that you and Donna . . . definitely knew each other. In fact, he said you may have been more than friends. That true?

Jay let out a long and frustrated breath.

Jay: It's true.

Me: Jay, why'd you lie to me?! We need to know everything you know, it's the only way this is going to work!

Jay: I'm sorry, Mo. I just . . . I just didn't want to scare you and Mom. Give you another reason to think I'm guilty. Everyone already does.

Mo: How'd y'all meet?

Jay: Mo, I can't talk about this over the phone. They're listening. Come on, I need you to be smarter than that.

I froze, unsure of what even to say. Jason wasn't cooperating the way I needed him to and it was bothering me. Coop looked at me and I just shook my head. I was done.

Coop: Look, man, we're knee-deep in some serious stuff. Donna, Rah, and he's even talking about a connection to the police. What's happening? Did you know she was a cop?

Jay: No, I swear. She told me her birth name was Donna, but I didn't know she was a cop till I got locked. I found out from my lawyer.

Coop: What about the name Viper? That ring a bell? Rah said Donna had intel on a confidential informant hanging around.

The rambling that came out of Jay's mouth next frightened me. I hadn't heard my brother sound that desperate since—well, since ever.

```
Jay: It doesn't ring a bell, but a rat makes
perfect sense. Coop, Mo, you have to believe
me. I didn't do this. I'm being framed. And if
the COs in here find out Donna was one of their
own, I'm dead. You hear me? Dead! Dane's in
here, too, now. Caught selling stolen shit.
I'm afraid he might even turn on me. The walls
are closing in. I need y'all to move faster!
```

I looked over at Coop, who had gone quiet. His eyes were darting all over the place and I could tell his mind was wandering. Something Jay said caught his attention, I just wasn't sure what it was.

I wanted to ask Jay more about Rico's whereabouts, but there was no point, he wouldn't answer. Especially not on monitored phones. But I had to get the info out of him somehow.

```
Me: We are, Jay, but we need to find the
person who gave you up. It's got to be the guy
who handed you the gun.
```

Jason went quiet.

```
Me: We know who it was. Rico, right?
Jay: That rat! I told him to just stay put
```

at his baby mom's house till this all blew over. He ain't the brightest. The cops will definitely flip him.

I looked over at Coop and we shared a knowing nod. I hated lying or even spreading the rumor that Rico was snitching, but I had to get the info somehow.

Jay: Look, I can't say anymore over the phone. It's not safe. I gotta go. Just please, find out something that can help. And hurry! I'mma keep my eyes out for Rico in here.
Me: Jay, wait!
Machine: Your call has ended . . .

CHAPTER NINETEEN

COOPER
RICO

What the hell? I thought to myself as Mo stared at her phone. I wasn't sure why Jay would mention the other guys over the phone. Maybe he was sending me a message? I was doing everything I could to free him. To free us.

But all any of those cops had to do was put two and two together and I would be the next one on their roster, just like Dane. Or would Dane give me up?! Jay was no snitch, but I barely knew Dane and what he was capable of. The cops could be coming to my door any minute.

My chest tightened and I had pins and needles in my legs. To make matters worse, my stomach was doing a bunch of backflips and I thought I might throw up.

Mo clasped the sides of her head and I could tell it was throbbing from this investigation. Hell, mine was, too.

My immediate fears for my own freedom were quickly replaced with the need to make sure she was okay. I left the garage, tripping on the single step that led into the hallway behind the kitchen. I got a glass of water and made a beeline for the bathroom, popping the vanity open and rummaging through

Dad's seemingly endless pill bottles for anything that remotely resembled a pain reliever.

Found it.

I got back to Mo as fast as I could and handed her the glass of water. She was already sitting on the ground with her legs curled up to her chest.

"Take these." I handed her two film-coated white pills.

Mo threw the pills back and chugged the whole glass of water.

"You know," Mo said, looking up at me, "I think I was dehydrated."

"Water helped, huh?" I asked.

"Yeah." She chuckled. "Welp, good news is we have a lead on Rico. Bad news is Jay was for sure hooking up with Donna."

"Yup." I sighed, leaning my head back against the wall. "Doesn't help his case," I slipped.

Mo cut her eyes at me but didn't say anything. We were both thinking it.

I realized just how bad this whole situation was. Especially now that Jay wasn't the only one in police custody. With them bagging Dane, I knew the walls were closing in. More arrests meant the cops probably knew who Jay was with that day. They would likely be taking us down one by one as they figured out our identities. That meant either me or Rico would be next. Unless I could get to Rico first and figure out what he knew.

Him handing Jay the pistol. The anonymous tip. The snitch hanging around that Rah mentioned. It was all connected. Who else knew Jason would have that gun other than me, Dane, and Rico? I took a deep breath.

Mo was right about the good news—now that we knew where Rico was hiding out at, it wouldn't be long before we got some answers.

I looked over at Monique and instantly the noise in my head calmed down. I watched her as she sat there with her eyes shut. There was one thing that could be said about Monique Simms. No matter how tired she was—no matter how stressed, frustrated, sad, angry, or just plain defeated she felt—she was breathtaking.

They say love tints your eyes to a shade of rose color. All I knew was that she was mesmerizing and I was starting to think that shooting my shot was quickly becoming a now-or-never deal. We hadn't had this much time together since ninth grade.

"Okay, let's regroup. Even though Peters's story checks out, meaning he didn't pull the trigger, he could still be involved, right? I mean it sounded like this information Donna had could've implicated not just Peters but his boss, even his whole precinct. I mean, this corruption could go all the way up to the mayor."

Chills ran up my spine. We were in the middle of a real investigation that could implicate a crooked police system. I thought back to DeAndre Joshua and Darren Seals, dudes a little older in Ferguson, Missouri, who'd testified against the police in the murder of Mike Brown. Like Samir, Mike Brown was killed by an officer in 2014. Both witnesses ended up brutally assassinated, killed in the exact same way.

It felt like Mo and I were in the middle of that same situation. Even though that realization made this whole ordeal all the more frightening, it made it feel more important, too. We needed to do this to possibly save more Samirs and Mike Browns in the future.

"But before we get overwhelmed with that, let's find Rico. He might be able to fill in some holes for us," Mo said with confidence. She pulled out her laptop and got to sleuthing. "Okay, here's Rico's socials . . . and here is a picture with his family. Cute kid but I don't recognize the mom."

I looked down at the photo of Rico holding his three-year-old daughter with his child's mother. He looked so happy. Much different from the way I saw him when everything went down.

"Go to her page right quick," I said.

Mo scrolled through the photos of Rico's girl. It's crazy all you can learn about a person from just their online profiles. Her birthday, where she worked, what car she drove; you could piece together someone's whole life from a few photos.

"Stop," I called out. "Look, all of these photos seem to be from the same park. You recognize it?"

"Yeah, actually, it's Turkey Thicket. I used to cheer there. Isn't far from here. She probably lives in the area."

"Okay, let's keep scrolling."

Mo delivered a couple more swipes when my eyes narrowed in on a photo of the woman braiding her daughter's hair on a porch.

"Right there. Zoom in, top right corner."

As Mo zoomed in, the numbers on the very top of the picture became clear. 1906.

"Coop, great eyes!"

"Thanks." I blushed. "But we still don't know the street."

"Well if I just . . . ," Mo muttered, typing away. "Boom! There's only one 1906 address in a five-mile radius. Tenth Street."

"Well would you look at that, we're getting pretty good at this," I said with a big goofy grin I desperately wanted to hide. Although, Mo cheesing back made me feel all the better.

"Let's go find Rico."

"Let's," Mo said, standing up.

But she must have stood up a little too quickly because she almost fell straight back down. I caught her just in time, but the glass didn't make it.

CRASH!

"Oh, Coop, I'm so sorry," she began.

That glass was the furthest thing from my mind. Suddenly I was holding Mo so tightly that my knees felt weak. The scent of her pomegranate body wash wafted through my nostrils and I tried to keep myself from melting into a puddle at her feet.

She looked up at me and there was just no hiding what was written across my face. But instead of recoiling or pulling away, she seemed to become just as lost as I was. We were drowning in each other's eyes, desperate for a breath that would only come if it passed between our lips.

Then she looked away.

"Sorry—I—you okay?" I stammered as I let go of her and knelt down to pick up the larger pieces of glass that were strewn across the floor.

"Yeah," she said, bending down to help me.

"No, I got this," I said. "We don't want you falling over again."

I laughed in what was my best attempt to clear the thick tension from the air.

"Yeah." She laughed awkwardly herself.

What was that? Did she want what I did? Was there really something here?

I tried to process it all. But then my imagination started conjuring up images of what might've happened if we hadn't pulled apart.

"You good?" Mo asked, and I realized I had just been kneeling there lost in my thoughts.

"Yeah—uhm." I cleared my throat. "Let me just put this in the trash and then we can head out."

Seconds after that, we were out the door.

The evening air warmed us both up, offering a stark contrast to the chill morning that had sent Mo practically running through my front door. Nestled in the heart of our own neighborhood, it was safe to say that we both felt the pressure mounting as we staked out the street looking for a potential police informant and backstabbing murderer.

We had managed to find street parking that kept us in the shadows of a tree as we watched the flow of people on the block.

"Someone's coming out of the building," she said. "Is that Rico? I can't see."

"Just a little old lady," I joked.

Mo laughed and relief washed over me once again. We sat in silence for a minute and the romantic tension in the air was stiffening again. It was all beginning to be a little too much to keep my feelings under wraps. The electricity of the hunt wasn't exactly helping.

My nerves were a wreck as I thought of what to do and what not to do—retract my hand quick enough to not let the feeling linger, but not fast enough that she would think that I was repulsed by her touch.

Shit! Why is this so hard?

I pulled my hand back slowly, and for a moment, the air in the car crackled with unspoken desires.

But Mo grabbed my hand and locked her fingers between mine.

Is she for real? Is this happening?

I looked up at her and was met with her eyes searching mine for a reaction. I knew right then and there that the moment in the garage wasn't in my head. She wasn't just faint from dehydration.

I outlined every feature, every dimple in her skin, and every tiny curl along her forehead. She was the picture of perfection and I wanted nothing more than to reach out and cup her face in my hands. My eyes lowered to hers and then to her lips and, for a second, I imagined what a stolen kiss might taste like. Both of us were leaning in now until we were mere inches from one another. I could feel her breath on my lips and I could have sworn I could hear her heart beating to the rhythm of mine.

And just when I thought we would both fold like lawn chairs, someone else caught my eye.

My eyes shot straight to the person walking down the street, ripping myself away from Mo's embrace.

"Oh shit," I whispered.

It was Rico.

CHAPTER TWENTY
COOPER
VIPER

I felt the whiplash of going from an intimate moment with Mo to spotting Rico.

My blood was at a slow simmer as I watched Rico, and thoughts began to cloud my judgment. Could he really be the snitch Rah mentioned? Snitching wasn't bad on its face. If we were so lucky to find out who killed Donna, I'd 100 percent be snitching. But I had nothing to do with that crime.

What made snitching bad was when people engaged in a crime together and one of the individuals told on the others to save themselves. It wasn't honorable. By street logic or otherwise. A solider wouldn't give up another solider in the face of war. If Rico had violated that, he'd be labeled a rat. I just hoped that wasn't the case, for Jay's sake and mine.

I was so eager for answers I didn't even turn the car off. I hopped out and marched across the street.

BEEP-BEEP!!

An old Chevy blared its horn as it swerved around me, nearly hitting me. For a split second I was frozen in place, but Rico barely looked back and kept moving. He was a man on a mission. Mo walked up behind me and handed me the keys to the car.

"Easy, Coop," she whispered, rightly so.

But I needed to get to him first. I needed to control the conversation so he didn't say anything that might reveal the truth to Mo.

We followed him slowly, doing our best to stay hidden. Up close, we could see he had headphones on, which made the tail job a lot easier.

"Oh snap." Mo nudged me and nodded to the back of Rico's arm. "You see that? Right elbow?"

My eyes searched Rico's arm and I almost had to laugh from disbelief. There, wrapped around Rico's elbow and down to his wrist, was a tattoo of a snake with sharp fangs and brown circular patches. I had noticed Rico was tatted up before, but I never took the time to clock every piece of art on his body.

"That look like a viper to you?" Mo asked.

"Sure does," I said, my blood growing from a simmer to a boil.

Rico went in his pocket for keys, and I knew we were nearing his house. We had to act.

"What's the plan, Coop?"

The question caught me off guard. I hadn't thought that far.

"Hang back," I said, quickening my pace behind Rico and leaving Mo trailing.

"Wait—" she started. But it was too late, I was locked in. I begged my adrenaline to do something useful other than making my hands shake with fury.

"Ayo, Rico!" I yelled when I was within range.

"What's goo—?" Rico began as he stopped and turned around. "Cooper?"

"Yeah, man, where you been? Ain't seen you around since Jason got bagged."

"Why you think? 'Cause shit been hot," Rico said, looking around. "They bagged Dane, too. What's up? Why you rolling up on me with some sort of energy?"

"But they ain't bag you?"

"Fuck you tryna say? They ain't bag you, either," Rico said, squaring up with me. He had a point there, but I couldn't even respond because of the fear and guilt surging through me. I looked over my shoulder to see Mo still a half block away. I didn't think she'd heard him, but the uncertainty had my heart thumping.

"I'm talking about—" I stopped speaking as I noticed Mo come up beside me. I had been about to mention Rico giving Jason the gun, which would definitely make Mo suspicious of me.

"They got an anonymous tip about Jason. About the gun he had," I said instead, trying to signal to the man. "I think you may know something about that . . . VIPER."

Rico's eyes swelled up enough to tell me everything I needed to know. He was caught.

"Rico, don't tell me you're the snitch. Jay has been such a good friend to you!" Mo said, stepping up.

"Mo, I can explain—" he started, going from aggressive to defensive. "Shit got out of control and I got boxed into a corner. When me, Jay, Dane, and—"

I didn't let him finish—I couldn't. Instead, I swung on him.

My fist connected with his jaw, sending him doubling backward. His face was the picture of shock as he stood there.

"Yo, what the fuck is your problem?" he yelled before lunging at me. Even though Rico was definitely bigger and likely way tougher than me, I had enough heart and anxiety coursing through me to supply at least three men with fighting spirit. I wasn't happy with Rico, but I played it up to justify attacking him.

"You're Viper?! How could you do this to Jason!" I shouted, my hands on his collar as we tussled on the concrete. I didn't even know how I ended up with my knees on his chest.

I could hear the faint sound of Mo's voice in the background.

"Cooper, I can't have you locked up, too!" Her words cut through the air when I finally calmed down enough for my brain to decipher what she was saying. "Come on!"

She was pleading at that point and I couldn't stand to hear that fear in her voice.

"Please," she whispered. "Not here. Not now."

I pulled myself to my feet and peeled that punk off the ground with me.

"Let's have a talk," Rico said between catching his breath. "But we gotta keep it down. My daughter is asleep."

"Cool, let's talk," I spat back.

Rico marched to his front door and we followed.

Mo grabbed my arm, her eyes darting between me and Rico as he opened the door. She had never seen this side of me. *I* had never seen this side of me.

"Coop, you sure about going in there? What if he's . . . you know . . . dangerous?" she whispered.

"I doubt he'll do anything with his daughter in the house, but you can stay out here so at least one of us could get help if needed. We're close, Mo; I can feel it. If we want to save Jay, I need to go through that door." And I meant it. For the first time, I felt this case was no longer about saving myself. I wanted to save Jason. Or I at least wanted the truth.

"Then I'm going with you," Mo said, looking up at me with those beautiful brown eyes. Part of me wanted her to stay outside to stay clear of any slip-ups by Rico, but the other part of me felt good that Mo was down to ride with me and for me.

All the more reason she couldn't find out my secret. She'd be crushed. Inside, the place was dimly lit with very little furniture. All I could see was a small couch and a TV atop a worn coffee table. The walls were stained yellow, the air was stale, the carpet worn. I felt a little for him. Rico was living like a man who'd do anything to get a leg up.

"Talk. Now," Mo insisted.

Her voice was low and growling, almost unrecognizable. Rico's eyes moved between the two of us, his hands raised in a defensive posture. If it was a fight he wanted, he would get it. And he probably needed to be more worried about Mo than me.

"Look, I don't know that woman who got shot, and I don't know about any anonymous tip," he shot back. "Jason is my boy." Rico's gaze flickered, a bead of sweat forming on his forehead.

"So, were you working with her partner, David? Did he have you pull the trigger?" Mo asked.

"Whoa, whoa! I didn't shoot anyone!" Rico protested. "I swear. We just went down there to loot and—"

"Enough with the BS, dog. You're Viper," I cut in quick. I needed to keep Rico from giving me up. I had to get him to focus on his connection to Donna. "You're the snitch Donna was on to. You were working with her ex-partner. He killed her and had you pin it on Jay!" I demanded, punching my fist into my hand.

Rico's gaze shifted, guilt etched across his face. "Okay, I am Viper, but that has nothing to do with Donna, or Melissa, or any ex-partner," he said.

"Are you serious right now? You're an informant?" Mo's eyes narrowed and she cocked her head to the side. She was starting to feel how I felt and if she got mad, I'd be the last of Rico's worries.

"I had no choice," he gasped as he plopped down on the flimsy couch. "A cop came to me about a week before the protest—said he had some shit on me that would send me away for twenty. He promised me that they'd wipe my record clean if—"

"If you pinned a murder on my brother," Mo cut in.

"No! Not a murder!" Rico quickly added. "Possession. The cop wanted me to give Jay a piece."

"A piece?" Mo asked.

"A gun. Said it was just to get him for holding, enough to twist his arm about something else altogether. Some shit I knew nothing about. Jason wasn't supposed to get jail time. The cop went so far as to say, if Jason didn't flip, he'd get a few months' probation and we'd be good. That's nothing, a slap on the wrist for Jay in exchange for twenty years of my life. It sounded like a good deal! No one was supposed to get killed. And I never called in any anonymous tip. I didn't have to. I'm thinking the cops already knew he had the gun."

Mo and I looked at each other. It was a good point. If the cops had Rico give Jay the gun, they wouldn't need a tip.

"And when did you give him the gun?" Mo asked to clarify.

"Right before the riot," Rico said, turning to me. "When we—"

"You mean you, Rico, Dane, and the other guy?" I jumped him.

Rico tilted his head in slight confusion for a split second as we locked eyes. The look on my face said it all. I needed him to help me out.

"Yeah, exactly," Rico said, staring me down.

"Were you with him after?" Mo asked.

"Nah, we split up. I didn't see what happened once we dipped back to the block."

The brief silence that followed should have been enough for me to realize gears were turning in Mo's head, but I was too caught up in the heat of the moment. Before I knew it, the words that I was hoping to never hear escaped her lips.

"Who else was with you that day, Rico?" Mo asked. "We know Dane was there, who's now arrested. Who was the other person?"

Her question hung in the air and my ears rang as time slowed down. Beads of sweat crowded my forehead as I tugged at my lucky bracelet.

"Apparently he doesn't know, either," I huffed.

"Let him talk, Coop," Mo spat back. I could tell she was beginning to get annoyed by my constant interrupting.

Rico looked at me and I looked right back, raising a single eyebrow, almost begging him to keep his mouth shut.

"I don't know the other dude. They was just there," Rico whispered, lowering his gaze.

A wave of relief washed over me.

"I never thought it would end like this," he continued. "I feel crazy about the whole thing. You got to believe me. I know what I did was fucked up, but I got a daughter, man. I wasn't trying to go back. You ain't got no idea what it's like inside."

I started to feel for Rico even more since he held me down, but Monique wasn't buying it.

What I knew for sure was that somebody wasn't telling the truth. If Rico was Viper, but didn't know Donna, how and why had Donna mentioned him to Rah?

"Who's behind this, Rico? Who ordered you to set Jason up?" Mo demanded.

"I don't know. The cop's face was covered when we met and it was dark. That's the beginning and end of it all. It was just the once," he insisted.

"Any distinguishable features?" I asked. "Black, white, tall, short?"

"He was a bigger guy. Sounded Black, but I could be wrong. And it was awkward. He had me sit in the back of an unmarked car. We were never face-to-face."

It was a lot to take in. I wanted to believe Rico but like this whole mystery, each answer led to more questions. And while we were trying to uncover the truth, who knew what lies we were being fed, and by who.

One thing was certain. Pops was right. *There's no honor among thieves.*

"I just can't believe you, Rico," Mo said as she headed for the door. The tone in her voice was the exact tone I couldn't bear to have her direct toward me. Like she was disgusted just being in the same vicinity as this person who had disappointed her.

"Mo, I'm sorry!" Rico called out. But it was too late, she was gone. I looked at him and shook my head as I turned for the exit.

"Don't act like you perfect, li'l bro," Rico called as I started to leave. "We all got secrets."

CHAPTER TWENTY-ONE
MONIQUE
QUESTIONS

After Coop and I confronted Rico, I just had to go home and rest. I needed a break from the investigation. I was tired mentally, physically, and emotionally. But I could barely sleep because I had so many questions on my mind. Like, *what was that look between Coop and Rico?*

And then that line I'd overheard, "We all got secrets." What the hell was that supposed to mean?

There was something strange going on and no one could tell me otherwise. My mind was playing tricks on me—it had been the whole day, but this was definitely something. I wasn't hallucinating, nor was I overreacting. Coop had been acting strange lately, in more ways than one, and I needed to know why.

Ever since the start of this thing I'd been trying to figure out one missing piece. Who was the fourth looter with Jason? It seemed odd to me that nobody knew him. And I couldn't even ask Jason because of his dang *code of silence*.

Coop didn't have any reason to lie to me, but for some reason

I felt he wasn't being entirely truthful. Looking back, I realized we had done everything in this investigation together—except confront Dane. *Why'd he do that without me?* Maybe I was just being paranoid.

Then again, why had he pulled back every time I reached for him when he seemed just as into me as I was into him? Wasn't he seeing the signs that I had been giving him—even before Jay was arrested? Hadn't he seen how much I wanted to be with him?

Now more than ever, he was my source of comfort. It had become so clear to me that one of the reasons—if not *the* reason— that I turned to him in my times of need was because I could trust him. Out of everyone around me, I could depend on him to carry me through a park with a huge gash on my face or to wipe my tears when some asshole had broken my heart. It was always him and, in a messed-up kind of way, it took Jay landing himself behind bars for me to realize it.

I just hoped Coop wouldn't break my heart. I hoped there wasn't *secrets* he was keeping from me because I truly believed we were in this together.

Regardless of my own feelings, there were more *pressing issues* to deal with. The fact that one of Jay's friends had helped frame him for Donna's murder was wild. I hated to admit it, but Mom was right. None of the people that Jay hung out with were good news. All of them except for Coop.

CHAPTER TWENTY-TWO

COOPER
WILD, WILD THOUGHTS

The day after confronting Rico, my body ached. It felt as if I had been running a mile a minute for days on end. I was tapped out. I just wanted to lie down and sleep uninterrupted for one night. But between thoughts of Mo and thoughts of prison, I couldn't shut down.

I could see she was growing impatient, too.

That evening Mo and I decided to discuss everything. But really we just wanted each other's company. Or at least, I just wanted hers.

"Hurts, huh?" Mo asked as she watched me clutch my bruised fist.

"It's definitely not something I'd recommend." I grinned a little.

She laughed. But it wasn't her regular laugh. She was holding back. Even with all the drama that we had gone through recently, she was always on a high frequency. Not only that, but she almost always laughed at my jokes. On the off chance that she didn't, she would be laughing at how weak my joke was instead. This, though—this wasn't a laugh. This was a forced chuckle. Something to try to cut through the awkwardness hanging between us.

"So, Rah claims it wasn't him . . . ," Mo began.

"And same goes for everyone else," I added.

"Of course it does. We can't take any of this at face value. Dane has an alibi. I think it probably holds since there hasn't been any news about him being connected to the murder. We confirmed Peters's alibi with the police station, but he could still be connected. Rico is still on my list. Something doesn't smell right about him being tied to framing Jay, and I'm wondering if Peters was the cop that confronted him."

"That was my thought, too."

"And then there's still our mystery guy who was at the scene with Jay and company moments before it all went down."

"And Rah," I said, deflecting.

"Yeah, but he gave us info that panned out, like Rico being Viper, so it seems doubtful."

"True."

"I feel like there's a piece we're missing. Something we're not considering."

I had my ideas and one of them made me turn cold.

There was always the possibility that Jay was in fact the one responsible for Donna's death. As I thought about it a little more, the what-ifs crept in faster than I wanted them to.

What if he saw her with another dude?

What if he realized she was a cop?

What if the gun went off accidentally?

Mo said she had seen her brother's face and would've known if he was lying. But he'd lied to her during this investigation and she was none the wiser.

It was hard to tell. As people grow, sometimes they change. Jason certainly wasn't the Jay I knew as a kid.

"We can't speculate too much right now," I said when I finally rolled back into reality. "We have to keep putting one foot in front of the other. No assumptions. Okay?"

"Okay." She sighed.

It was weird being the guide at that point. Mo had always been our fearless leader. I was the Robin to her Batman. But clearly she needed a breather, so I had to step up.

So that begged the question, what was our next move? It felt like we'd hit a dead end.

My thoughts turned back to Jay. I recalled Mo's statistic about the percentage of women murdered by their partner. I didn't say it out loud, though. I didn't need to; I'm sure Mo was thinking the same.

Even if he didn't pull the trigger, he should've seen something, I thought. *What if Jay was more involved in this than he's letting on?*

"Coop, I need to ask you something." Her words cut through my silent brainstorm.

"What's up?"

"You weren't down there with Jason, were you? That day? I just keep thinking about who else Jason is cool with from the neighborhood and I keep coming up with you. And then there seemed to be something with you and Rico, or even you and Jay on the phone."

It was a question that was long overdue. I had held it together pretty good up until this point, but I could feel a bead of sweat trickle down the back of my neck.

She was perceptive and smart and I felt absolutely terrible for lying to her. But I wasn't hiding anything that could break open our investigation and I truly wanted Jason free just as bad as she did. At this point, the truth would only hurt our cause more than help it.

At least that's what I told myself.

"No, of course not, Mo," I said, looking her right in the eyes. Mo nodded.

"Cool, just making sure. Whew, I need a break," she said, getting up and heading out the back door, making herself comfortable on the new deck chairs that Dad had bought at the beginning of summer. Relief washed over me and I went to the kitchen to look for something to eat. The pantry had a couple bags of chips. The fridge was my next stop and I grabbed a bottle of soda before getting two glasses and making my way out back to meet Mo. She had reclined the deck chair and was staring up at the sky, which was changing to shades of pink. It was the last of the afternoon sun and for a minute everything felt calm.

It was like one of those déjà vu moments, where you feel like you've been in a place and time before, but you definitely haven't. I felt like I was right where I was meant to be.

The evening sun bathed the backyard and the light breeze blanketed us both. The air was thick with the scent of summer, and the distant hum of the city filled the silence.

"Ooh, snacks!" Mo said, grabbing a bag out of my hand and popping it open.

"You're welcome—I guess." I laughed.

"I know," she said with a mouth full of salted chips.

She had a crumb on her lower lip and I couldn't help but laugh. Her cheeks were filled like a little hamster and her tired eyes had a sparkle that I missed. She looked more like the playful girl I had known my whole life.

"Don't forget to breathe," I teased as I sat down at the end of her chair.

"Boy"—she smirked at me—"shut up! You know I'm greedy."

We both laughed as she set the bag down and took a glass of soda from my hand. After a brief sip, she laid back on the chair and continued her sky-gazing.

"You know, Coop, it's crazy how everything we've been through ties back to this messed-up system."

"Yeah." I nodded, pausing to take a swig from my glass. "It's like we're fighting against something bigger than just the people involved."

I waited for a response, but it didn't come, so I looked over at Mo. Her eyes were reflective—filled with a mix of frustration and sadness.

"When this all started," Mo began, "it was about Samir. That's what we rallied for. Yet I haven't even spoken to his mom since the shooting. I've been so focused on my own problems that I've forgotten Samir. Maybe he's been forgotten by so many already. Another Black boy killed, and what? We move on like it never happened. Why does this keep happening? Why won't this place change?"

The weight of Monique's words settled between us, a heavy acknowledgment of a reality we couldn't escape. My gaze shifted to the skyline, my mind absorbing the magnitude of our collective struggle in the city. Mo's words were true but highlighted something powerful about Rah and even Jason's rhetoric. If we wanted different results, we had to do something different. Not necessarily violence, but if not, what?

"Maybe they figure if they keep getting us riled up about a new thing, we'll forget the last thing we were angry about in the first place. It's how they've planned things for decades, centuries . . ."

"Yeah, it's definitely a design. That's why they call it 'the Trap,' right?" she seconded.

"Exactly."

Mo took the words right out of my mouth. In fact, she probably took them out of my subconscious where I didn't even know they existed until they danced across her lips.

"We can try all we want and do the best that we can to bring justice to these crises," Mo said, "but we can't forget to live."

See what I mean?

She turned to look at me and, for the first time, I knew what was dancing around in *her* subconscious. I knew exactly what she wanted to say but couldn't bring herself to. She was a strong young woman and strong young women aren't going to be seen begging for no man's attention—not even ones that they trust.

She wasn't pulling back. She was waiting for me not to.

So, I stopped.

I stopped trying to contain what I had felt for her since we were kids—what I so badly hoped she had felt, too. My stomach flipped as I worked up the nerve to do what was on my mind. The air became charged with electricity that mirrored the current running between us. I knew she could feel it, too, because she was silent. I could see her watching me. Our eyes tracing the outlines of each other's silhouette.

In that moment, the boundary between friendship and something more blurred. My eyes must have extended an unspoken invitation because Mo leaned in and I did the same. The world around us faded into the background as the sparks of the investigation and shared desire intertwined. It was a moment suspended in time, a release of pent-up emotions.

When our lips met, it was exactly as I had always envisioned it. I had to pull away for a second just to make sure she was real. She looked at me with the biggest doe eyes, waiting for confirmation. So I gave it to her.

I leaned back in and pressed my lips against hers. They were soft and fit perfectly against mine. She seemed to leap into my arms and straddle me as I pulled her in and my hands fell to her hips. I felt her hands reach under my shirt and press against my ribs, making their way to my chest. My fingers found their way to her back where her skin was soft as butter.

She was perfection.

As we pulled away, breathless and exhilarated, the backyard seemed transformed. The stars above shone a little brighter, and the weight of our struggles felt momentarily lifted.

"Should we go to your room?" she asked softly.

My brain almost jumped out of my head imagining what was about to happen next, but I didn't panic. Instead, we stood as I took her hand to lead her inside.

Tonight, my wildest thoughts were about to come true.

CHAPTER TWENTY-THREE

MONIQUE
DISCOVERIES

That morning, I was on cloud nine. He wanted to be with me and I wasn't just imagining it. There had to be a reason why he had been holding back before. But none of that mattered now. The important thing was that we felt the same way about each other and we were going to crack this case one way or another. Knowing that I had his support meant more to me than I could put into words.

I thought about our childhoods—the class bully that I'd saved him from in kindergarten and the one he saved me from in fourth grade. I thought about playing Uno with him in Mom's kitchen and how we'd laughed so much my belly ached. I remembered watching the tears roll down his cheeks as he'd struggled to breathe from fits of giggles and the tears he held back when we laid his mom to rest.

I remember how tightly he squeezed my hand that day.

We had been through so much in such a short space of time and the more I thought about it, the more I realized that I wouldn't change a single thing. I mean, I'd bring his mom back if I could, and of course I wouldn't have Jay sitting in jail in an alternate reality. But overall, there's nothing I would take back. Not a single word or tear or scar.

I picked up my phone to text him, but I quickly set it back down. I didn't want to be too hasty. I still had to be sure I wasn't being delusional. I knew exactly how the heat of the moment can make us do things we regret the next day.

Besides, just because Coop had made his feelings known, didn't mean that any of Jay's problems went away. I had to focus on getting Jay out of jail and finding the killer.

That brought me back to what Mom had said the night before when I got back home.

"The cops were in the neighborhood asking people questions about Jason and anyone who hung out with him."

From the looks of things, the MPD was rounding up as many young men from our neighborhood as they could get their hands on. Maybe the cops didn't have much evidence on Jay. All the more reason to keep digging.

Image after image splayed across the screen as I looked for clues among the footage I'd saved. I wasn't even sure what I was looking for, but there had to be something out of the ordinary—something that would ring the alarm bells in my head. I opened another folder that contained snaps of me and Coop over the years. My favorite one had to be the one of me, him, and his mom on my birthday, right here in this very house.

Suddenly I was grinning like an idiot as I sat alone in my room.

"Concentrate!" I ordered myself, closing the window and getting back to the footage . . . again.

This time, something caught my eye immediately. The files in that folder were numbered from one to eighty-one. I had gone over it three times to make sure that I had done it correctly.

Yet, number three was missing now.

I checked and checked again, and I couldn't find it.

I closed the window and thought for a second.

Hmm . . .

I clicked on the trash on my desktop and breathed a sigh of relief. There it was: file number three. I must've accidentally deleted it at some point.

I hit Restore and closed the trash folder, navigating back to the original folder. I clicked on the file and it opened up in the media player. That was the one. I had looked over it a few times, but racked my brain trying to remember how I had deleted it in the first place.

But soon that thought flew out of my head, replaced by a pounding in my chest.

Can't be. I double clicked the video a few times to zoom in closer.

"What the hell?" I whispered to myself as I realized how it had ended up in the trash. It felt surreal. Like I was in the middle of a nightmare. The room started to spin and I just needed to take a second to breathe.

I needed to talk to Cooper King.

CHAPTER TWENTY-FOUR
COOPER
CLOSING IN

Did that really happen?

I lay in my bed the next morning, smiling like a fool. I smiled so much my cheeks hurt and the corners of my lips pinched. I closed my eyes and flashed back to the night before—the look in Mo's eyes, the feeling of her skin beneath my fingertips, the heavy breathing and soft kisses.

I was lost in it, only to be jarred by rapping at the front door, followed by Dad shouting.

"What you doing on my property?" *This can't be good.*

I threw on some sweats and walked out into the hallway just as Dad called my name. My heart missed a beat when I entered the living room and came face-to-face with the uninvited guests.

Two cops, a young woman and an older man.

"Yeah?" I called back, forcing my feet to move forward when all they wanted to do was stay rooted to the spot. I felt like I couldn't breathe—like I was drowning in the stifling energy that was reverberating through the air.

"I'm Detective Hunter," said the young female cop. "And this is my partner, Detective Martin."

"They want to speak with you about Jason," Dad said with a scowl on his face. His back was turned to the cops at this point, and he was giving me the what-did-I-tell-you-about-messing-with-that-crowd scowl. I knew that look and resigned myself to my fate. In the event that I wouldn't get taken away in cuffs that morning, I was still going to get my fair share from Dad.

"What about him?" I asked Detective Hunter.

"Mind if we come in, Mr.—uhm?"

"Mr. King," Dad said bluntly.

The arrival of the officers shattered the fragile peace. The authoritative thud of their city-issued boots on the floor echoed through the quiet house like a harbinger of the trouble that had found its way to our doorstep.

"What can my son do for you?" Dad asked as he showed the cops to a seat in the living room.

"Like I said, I'm just here to ask a couple of questions. No one's in trouble . . . yet."

My nerves were on edge as I tried to keep up a facade of innocence. I was ready to let denial flow effortlessly from my lips like a practiced script, but I had to be sure to only answer the questions they asked. That was a little something Jay had told me years ago during my first scouting job for him:

If you get caught, DO NOT give them more than what they're asking for.

"Where were you on the day of the protest, young man?" Detective Martin asked.

"I was right here, on this couch."

"You weren't out looting with your friend, Jason Simms?" Detective Martin continued.

My mind was all over the place. I thought about all the stolen clothes just a few yards away up in my room. And I still had the THR1FT app on my phone with messages setting up an exchange of stolen goods.

I'd been sloppy. I'd been a fool. I was on the verge of being caught.

"No," I replied when I managed to calm my mind. "Like I said, I was right here on the couch."

"Well, a few people from the neighborhood were arrested last night," he continued in a very matter-of-fact way. "Some of them say they've seen you hanging around with Simms a lot leading up to the riot. And that you're always with his sister."

Despite the stakes at hand, him mentioning Mo set me off. "His sister is my best friend. We all grew up together. Is that a crime?"

"Coop," Dad said, warning me.

"No, Dad. I'm sick of these cops trying to pin things on innocent people. They're just looking for another Black kid to kill."

"Cooper!" he snapped.

The room fell silent as Dad looked at the officers, likely expecting them to cart me off to the pen. But they didn't do that. Instead, they stood up to leave and I realized that they had nothing more on me than the fact that I was friends with Jay.

"I hope you're telling the truth, kid. For your sake," Hunter said, seemingly unsatisfied with my responses. "Goodbye, Mr. King. I'll be in touch, Cooper," she finished, handing me a business card.

The moment the door shut I felt the weight of the truth pressing on me. I had tried to manage this problem all on my own, but now that the cops were literally and figuratively at my door, I decided it was time to come clean. I approached Dad with a heavy heart, more concerned with the disappointment I was about to cause him than the subsequent tongue-lashing I was bound to get.

"Dad, I need to tell you something," I said as I watched him lock the front door.

"Yeah, I'd say so. Start talking."

He wasn't going to make it easy.

"Well, it all started when my summer job got cut. Jason told me there was a way we could make some cash."

My dad just stared at me blankly so I kept going.

"By looting the stores on H Street during the protest."

"Jesus, Coop!" my dad blurted out, shaking his head. "So you were out there that day?"

I looked down at my feet and gave him a small nod.

"Cooper," Dad said, exasperation as clear as day in his tone. "What were you thinking? Didn't I tell you to stay away from the protest? If you needed money that bad you should've come to me. We could've figured something else out. But stealing—"

"Well, I wasn't supposed to be stealing. I was just supposed to be a lookout for Jay and his crew," I replied under my breath.

"You were what?!"

"Looking out for—"

"Oh, no, I heard you. I just wanted to make sure you could hear yourself. Are you insane, Cooper?"

"I'm sorry, Dad. I figured I could earn some extra money. I know things been tight around here with Mom—"

"Stop! Don't you say it. Have you ever wanted for anything? Have you ever gone without?"

"No, sir," I mumbled, hot tears forming in my eyes.

"Then I don't want to hear it!"

He was pacing now. He raised his hands over his head, balling them into fists and I was sure he was going to send me across the room.

"Did he do it?"

"Do what?"

My dad turned and charged at me. "Did Jason kill that woman? Were you there for that too?!"

"No! No, I wasn't there. I don't know what happened. And I don't think Jason did this."

"You don't think?"

"I don't know, Dad. We split up, but if you'll just let me–"

"No. I won't just let you, Cooper. From now on, I want to know where you are and what you're doing—AND with whom. At all times. That's the protocol for the rest of the summer. I'm not going to lose you, too!"

His words hung in the air as we stared at each other. I got it. For the first time since Mom had died, I got it. The way I felt about Mo was something like what he'd felt about Mom. Images of the way he looked at her, how they used to laugh together, came rushing back in. Mom's death had broken him and I was the last piece of her that he had.

I felt like shit.

"Dad, I . . . I'm sorry. I didn't mean for all of this to happen."

He was furious—his face mangled in a pained expression and I had no idea what else to say to him. An apology seemed so pointless and superficial but then his face softened.

"I just saw so much more in your future than this. I know you haven't exactly been dealt the greatest cards, but you always had your head on straight. I never felt like I ever really had to worry about the path you were on. I'm—"

He paused and left me in an uncomfortable silence and threw his arms around me.

"This is on me, Dad, not you."

He pulled back and placed his hand on my shoulder, looking down at the floor between us, as if willing it to open up and swallow him. He wiped his tears with his free hand. The weight of his disappointment hung in the air.

"Coop, listen to me," he spoke calmly as he raised his eyes to meet mine, his tall frame still slightly hunched over. "We need to face this head-on. We're marching down to the police station, and you're going to tell them the truth. I raised a leader, not a follower. So, you're going to lead the way by coming clean."

"Dad, please," I pleaded urgently. "Just give me some time. I can figure this out. I believe Jason is being framed. I just need to find out who's behind all of it. All the pieces are there, I know it. There's something I'm not seeing. I promise, I'll tell the cops, but I need to clear Jay's name."

"No," Dad said resolutely. It was such a firm no that it knocked the wind out of me. "But you have until I can get in touch with a lawyer that'll take this on, because it's looking like we'll need one. Don't make me regret this, Cooper."

I nodded. The heat was officially on.

PING!

It was a text from Mo. A few moments ago I thought things couldn't get any worse, but they just had.

Shit.

CHAPTER TWENTY-FIVE

COOPER
SECRET'S OUT

Mo: What the fuck Coop???????!!!!

Right below that was a snapshot of me . . . brand-new Supreme duffel slung over my shoulder . . . and the bracelet my mom gave me shining in the sun. It was from the video I'd tried to delete. I knew right then and there that I should have left well enough alone. Now that she had caught me trying to delete the clip, she would know that I had been trying to hide this the entire time.

"Dad, can I head out?" I asked, turning to my dad with a desperate look on my face.

"Did you hear what I said?" Dad scoffed. "You're not going anywhere."

"Without telling you where I'm going or who I'll be with. I'm going to Mo's and I will not be going anywhere else from there. Just straight to Mo's and straight back home," I said, my tone practically begging. "Please, Dad. Just trust me."

"Trust you?" My dad laughed. "You become a comedian all of a sudden?"

My face remained unchanged. I wasn't going to back down from this one. She needed to hear this from me—face-to-face. With those cops going around the neighborhood questioning people, who knew what they would tell her if they headed her way.

"Please," I repeated. "I lied to her. I told her I wasn't at the protest when . . . well, you know the truth now. She deserves to hear it, too. You said be a leader, right? Come clean? This is the first step."

My dad put his hand to his chin, thinking. "You're going to find a way to get to her either way, aren't you?" Dad sighed.

"Yes."

I was done with the lies and he wouldn't have believed them anyway.

"Go." He shrugged.

"Thank you, thank you."

"Straight back home!" he shouted out the door behind me. "And open those blinds on the way out so I can see you from here."

I took off running. I could see her doorstep from mine, but it felt like I was stuck in one of those nightmares where your legs were sinking in quicksand. My breath hastened and my heart was back to thumping like an 808. I peeped the drapes being drawn in her house.

She saw me.

I pulled my legs out of that imaginary quicksand faster than

I could blink. I was at her door a second after that, pounding as hard as humanly possible without breaking it down.

"Mo, can we talk?" I yelled.

I ducked off the porch and walked around to her window.

"MONIQUE! Can you just listen to me for a minute? I can explain everything, okay? Just let me explain!"

Dead silence. I had really screwed up. I should have been honest with her from the jump. I had broken her trust and I didn't know how I was ever going to be able to fix that. Would she even let me try?

"Mo, please, just let me in," I pleaded, leaning my forehead against her window.

I must have stood there for a good five minutes before I got the picture. She wasn't going to come to that window. I thought about heading back home.

But this wasn't just some girl. This was the girl that I loved—the girl that I had been in love with for most of my life. She was my soul tie—my other half. She was the one person for whom I was willing to put in all the effort.

So I walked myself back over to the porch and sat down.

"I ain't got nowhere else to be, Mo. I'mma be out here until your mom gets home. That's fine by me."

"And you think she's going to be impressed with her son's coconspirator sitting on her doorstep?" her voice boomed, but was a bit muffled from inside the house.

I looked around to make sure nobody was in earshot and then walked to the door to talk lower.

"You're not going to sell me out to your mom. You wouldn't break her heart like that."

"Oh yeah? Try me!"

"Fine! I will."

Monique Simms wasn't one to take anyone's bull, especially not mine. I was in for one long wait and I knew it. I gave up the idea that I could coax her out of the house and strapped myself in to serve my time on that porch. It was the least I could do to show her how sorry I truly was.

And I *was* truly sorry—not just because I had been caught in a lie, but because I should have known better all along. I felt like the idiot she probably thought I was at that moment and I couldn't blame her for it.

After all, it was my actions that had landed me there.

I waited. And waited.

And then, I waited some more.

Morning turned to midmorning and that gave way to midday, which hurried itself out the way for the afternoon. Still, I waited. Just when I thought I might give up, I heard shuffling come from inside and my ears perked up.

Finally, I thought, popping up from my seat.

But she was just walking around the kitchen—probably getting herself something to eat.

I carried on waiting, leaning my head on my knees to keep from falling asleep.

Then the door creaked open and I looked up just in time to see her glaring down at me with a mixture of anger and longing.

"I'm sorry," I said without trying to explain things away or sweep them under the rug. It was just another one of those things that Pops had taught me. Sometimes, when you're in the wrong, don't try to explain first. If a woman wants your explanations, she'll ask you for them. If you owe them to her, give them freely. But when you've messed up, start with sorry. Follow it with remorseful actions, and then wait for her to give you the green light.

"You're sorry, *but*?" Mo asked, folding her arms in front of her and cocking an eyebrow at me.

"No buts. Just sorry."

"You should be. I thought you were better than that, Cooper. How could you?"

"Listen, I didn't know things were going to get so far out of pocket. It's just . . . I needed the money because of the job cuts."

"So stealing was the answer?"

I dropped my head. I walked right into that.

"Answer me," she demanded.

"I—"

"You what? Cat got your tongue now? You were talking my ears off asking me to let you in. Now you're going to stand there in silence?"

I honestly didn't know what to say to her at that moment. It felt like all my words would sound hollow. This whole situation was all wrong. I had always known that it was wrong, but it was Jay. He was a big brother to me, too. And he was convincing. And no one was supposed to get hurt. And so many other things I didn't say because they'd all just sound like excuses.

"SPEAK, COOPER!" Mo demanded again.

"I messed up. What you want me to say, Mo? I already said I'm sorry, I shouldn't have been there."

Mo snorted and shook her head. "Cooper, being there is one thing, but lying to me this whole time about something so important is a whole other thing. I want you to explain that part."

But I had no explanation.

"You can't, can you?" She laughed, her voice dripping with anger and disappointment. "Forget it. Go on home, Cooper King. I've got nothing left to say."

She slammed the door in my face and I had no intention of trying to stop her or call out to her. Until I had a valid explanation or, at the very least, a way to make her see things from my perspective, there was no way she was going to listen to me.

To make matters worse, we didn't have much time until my own father expected me to serve up a different kind of explanation to the MPD.

I couldn't recall ever feeling so low. Even when Mom died, I had people around me. I had a sense of support and I felt like everything would find a way of working itself out. This was different—it was cold. I was being shut out from every which way and the people that I cared about now looked at me with so much disappointment. As if I was no more than a common thug.

I really messed up this time.

PART THREE
COMPLETION

CHAPTER TWENTY-SIX

COOPER
ALONE PT. 1

I walked back home with my tail between my legs, licking my wounds and feeling sorry for myself. I wanted to be mad at Mo. I wanted to stand there and talk about how she just didn't understand, but I'd only be fooling myself. She, of all people, understood what was what in these streets. She was the one fighting for things to change. To have stayed and tried to convince her that she *didn't* understand would have been an even bigger slap in her face. I accepted my fate and walked through the front door.

Dad was already gone, but there was a note.

Left for work. If you're reading this, you've come "straight back." Stay home, Cooper.

I sank into the solitary confinement of my room, the walls closing in around me as if the weight of impending doom pressed on my chest. The silence was agonizing. I picked up my phone, but there was no one to call. The only person who could bear the weight of what was going on was beyond mad at me and I didn't know if there was a way to change that.

I told myself that she needed some time to breathe, but how much time did I have left? The officer's questions still lingered in my mind, taunting me like an accusatory whisper in the silence of my room.

It's crazy: At the beginning of the summer I didn't know what I was passionate about. But investigating Donna's murder taught me so much about not just the city but myself. Donna died fighting for Samir and kids like him. Shoot, Donna died fighting for me. That inspired me. That lit something in me that I didn't realize was there. I was feeling passionate about being a revolutionary. But now I may never get the chance to live up to my full potential. If I were arrested, I'd just be another statistic. A Black boy who didn't get to see his prime. *Pine or steel*, just like my dad had told me.

Tendrils of doubt snaked through the air. I was beginning to think that jail was a real prospect for me. The fear that I would be implicated in a crime in which the truth had been bent so far out of shape was sickening. I felt my throat catch as I shut my eyes. Life had been so simple a few weeks ago. All I'd had to worry about was finding a summer job and having fun.

I thought about how many sunny days I had taken for granted and contrasted the possibility of spending countless other summers with Mo against the probability of being put away as an accessory to murder. A murder that was shrouded in ambiguity, no less. My mind sped through the narrative that had been painted by the police with brushstrokes that undoubtedly blurred the lines of truth. All to protect their own corruption.

And what about Samir?

Was Samir's death a tragedy as they claimed or a pawn in a larger, more sinister game?

Regret was a bitter and lonely friend that begged for company. The more I thought about the decision to follow Jason, the angrier I became. I replayed the events of the protest like a mental slideshow that stunk of consequences. I wished I could make it stop, but the images just kept going—over and over. The cracks in my armor had finally shattered.

"I should have stayed inside and listened to Dad," I said aloud to myself.

The harsh truth of my naivety cut through me like a knife. Dad's words were the caution that I needed to hear in a moment of blind allegiance to Jay, but they fell flat. And now they echoed in my mind. The burden of accountability settled on my shoulders and the heavy realization that I had messed up the one good thing I had pained me.

As the minutes dragged on, I found myself glued to the screenshot Monique had sent. My eyes flicked between the pixels and her message as I tried to decode the emotion behind the screen. Was she mad at me because I lied or was she angry that she had let me get close enough to hurt her? Maybe she was disgusted with me.

I read over all our messages, trying to relive the feeling of being happy and being a team before all of this had gone so wrong. I scrolled as high up as I could go and read each one out, focusing more on her responses in the thread than my own. I read all the way back down to the bottom.

Mo: What the fuck Coop???????!!!!

Then the image of me caught on camera, red-handed.

I should have just recognized the fact that I couldn't change anything, put my phone away, and started preparing for my eventual conversation with a bunch of cops down at the station. But when did I ever do what I was supposed to? Instead, I just kept staring at my phone. At that point, I was willing it to ping. I would have taken her being angry at me, yelling at me, and even cussing me out. Anything would have been better than silence.

Then, something in the screenshot caught my eye.

Hold up . . . that cop.

In the pic, way in the background, was the cop I collided with right after the gunshots. But this was from *before* I'd run into him—*before* Donna was murdered. Even though they wore the same balaclava mask as the rest of the officers, their uniform was slightly different. It was blue instead of black. It wasn't something I noticed that day, I could clearly see the difference now. And from what I could tell that he was heading in the direction the gunshots came from.

Toward Donna.

It didn't make any sense. All the police had been on the front lines of the protest, trying to quell the riots. They hadn't dispersed until the shots went off. What was this lone officer doing walking through the back streets during the protest?

The realization hit me like a lightning bolt, spotlighting the shadowy corners of my understanding. The cop, this ghostly figure, seemed to be making a beeline for the murder scene. If Donna was onto something big, the higher-ups were probably in on trying to keep things quiet. It could've been any cop out there assigned to dispose of the threat that was Donna Brown.

I looked closer at the image. The cop's balaclava hid his identity, but his badge was visible.

Gotcha.

I searched my drawer for a magnifying glass and held it up to the zoomed-in photo. I couldn't make out the numbers immediately but with some time, I'd be able to decipher them.

I gotta figure out who he is. What he's in on.

My room turned into a mission control hub, where the search for truth kicked off again. I got out my laptop and opened it up. When I hit the power button, the screen's luminescence hit me right in the eyes and I realized how long I had been lying on my bed. I looked around the room as the light slowly began to fade.

Sundown.

I hit my desk light. I went to the footage that Mo sent and started my own combing process, trying to find any images of the cop in the blue uniform I could. Different angles, distances and shots would help piece together the badge number he wore.

The road ahead was becoming sketchier by the second, but I had nothing and everything to lose. Something told me that all I needed to do was find the identity of this cop and my luck would change.

CHAPTER TWENTY-SEVEN
MONIQUE
ALONE PT. 2

PAIN

PAIN, *a four-letter word that defines my existence,*
A relentless force, offering no resistance.
Repeatedly stabbing, jabbing, grabbing at what's left of me
Breaking me down and scattering the rest of me.

PAIN, a journey through darkness with absolutely no end in sight,
Just a battle with shadows and no strength left to fight.
A prisoner of memories, I can't erase.
Bonded in chains by feelings I can't escape . . .

PAIN, a lesson in love I didn't deserve.
A heart once open, now forever reserved,
Betrayed I stand, amidst the ruins of our flame,
A soul engulfed by an unquenchable pain . . .

I sat alone in my room feeling like the life had been drained from my body by the queen of the damned herself. The sting of betrayal cut deep as I grappled with the harsh reality of Coop's actions. The trust that I had placed in him was completely shattered like fragile glass and the sharp shards had cut my heart. And all he had to show for it was a *sorry*. Imagine that. Imagine taking a delicate piece of china and throwing it on the ground, then expecting to piece it back together. Would the words *I'm sorry* fix it? Would anything be able to restore it back to what it was before the screwup?

The answer was a resounding *no*.

"How could he do this?!" My voice crawled out of me in a rasp. I had cried so much that day that I barely had anything left to let out.

Now, my mind replayed the moments leading up to the revelation, each memory tainted by the realization that Coop had been lying to me the whole time. I hated confronting the ache of betrayal and the realization that two of the most important men in my life had been the cause of so much anguish.

I thought we were in this together.

My feelings for Coop made me want to forgive him, but acceptance was too bitter a pill to swallow right then.

Not to mention the fact that there was another element of acceptance for me to contend with: Jason's guilt.

With more and more people being arrested on the daily, and now, the one person who I'd thought was innocent in all of this having some type of involvement, I didn't know what to believe. The fact remained that a young woman—a cop—had been shot on these streets and my brother was in the vicinity with a weapon that fit the bill. And they were connected. The line between truth and deceit was a tight one and I didn't know which side I was standing on.

There was another thought that I kept pushing way down deep. A thought I had been tiptoeing around this whole time.

Maybe Jason actually did it.

The admission hung in the air. It was a heavy acknowledgment that pierced through the layers of denial that I had been clinging to like a security blanket. My heart ached with a truth that I was reluctant to embrace. But I allowed myself to feel the pain, to confront the raw emotions that threatened to consume me. It was the only way for me to begin to see clearly again—to see through the betrayal that stood out like a gaping, jagged wound. I had to figure out the truth, whether it was a convenient truth or a world-shattering one.

If it was Jay, so be it. He made his bed. I'd allow justice to be served. But if it wasn't, I still wouldn't let him—or anyone else—rot in a cell over something they hadn't done.

I need to find out the truth, no matter how much it hurts. No matter where it led.

CHAPTER TWENTY-EIGHT

COOPER
NEW LEAD

My head hurt.

I hadn't slept a wink that night. My goal had been to find as much information as I could about the masked cop in the video, and I got caught up in trying to decipher his badge number. But I had no idea what the last digit was. Then again, uncovering three out of four of them wasn't bad. It was enough motivation to keep me going even when my eyes felt like they were on fire and the yawns came more frequently.

PING!

My phone demanded my attention and I have never so quickly obliged. I had hoped, somewhere deep down, that Mo would see things from my perspective or that she'd reach out and ask for me to wrap up this case with her.

I looked down at my screen.

You have 1 new notification.

Facebook, I read as my shoulders slumped, defeated.

I closed my eyes and squeezed them tight, light rings and

static forming behind my shut eyelids. In that moment of darkness, memories of Mom flooded my thoughts. I could almost hear her voice, that mix of stern yet loving cadence that echoed in the back of my mind.

Cooper, baby, remember the path you're on reflects not just on you, but on us, on our family.

The echo of her words sank deep into my mind and I couldn't help but wonder what she would say if she found out about my recent spat with Mo—or what I had been doing with Jay. In her words, I was "diving headfirst into a world of trouble." She always said that about kids in the neighborhood who had strayed too far from what their parents had taught them.

Would she be disappointed? Angry? I shook my head, trying to dispel the imaginary conversation, but her presence was there with me. I was likely punch-drunk from a lack of sleep, but it felt like she was standing right beside me.

I thought about what she would have said.

You're smarter than this, Coop. Don't let the streets drag you down.

I sighed, imagining her disapproving gaze. If she were here, she'd probably give me that look, the one that was a mix of concern and love. And then, she'd lay down some tough love, reminding me of the values she'd instilled in me.

I opened my eyes and the static behind my eyelids faded away. The room seemed quieter, and I couldn't escape the fact that, even in her absence, my mom's influence still hovered over me. The thought of disappointing her forced me to reassess the decisions I had made, and I couldn't help but wish for the strength to honor her memory through the right choices. I had let her down. I had let my father down. I had let Mo down.

I had to keep going if I was going to redeem myself.

It was 5:40 a.m. and after a night of combing through social media and googling ways to find someone's name based on their badge number, I was beat. As it turns out, the only way to really get your hands on that kind of information is to call or visit the police department and ask them who the person in question is. And since I wasn't taking myself down to the precinct prematurely, that was out of the question.

So, I sat there for a good couple of hours, trying random searches or staring into the eerie darkness around my laptop screen. My fingers had gone from dancing across the keyboard to finger-tapping as exhaustion set in.

Then, through all the brain fog, it hit me. If I only had one number to figure out, there were only ten possibilities from zero to nine. It pained me to think that it had taken me all night to reach that conclusion, but I could chalk it up to me being beyond tired.

Ten numbers were all that stood between me and the cop's identity, so I went back to Google and typed in:

Badge Number MPD 8931

From there, I tried 8932, then 8933—and on and on I went until 8938. Each number came back with little to no results, but 8938—that number sent me into a whirlwind of news articles.

One after the other, they all spoke of one man—a brave officer who'd been killed in action five years prior.

What the hell?

It was obviously impossible that it was the cop I'd run into at the protest. Unless they repurposed badges, which I figured maybe they did?

Still, I read on.

"Andrew McDonald of the MPD is survived by his wife, Sheila McDonald, and their son, Rahul McDonald."

We were literally investigating the murder of a police officer—could it be a coincidence that I had stumbled upon another murdered cop? Or did this have something to do with Donna?

As I read on, I learned that Officer McDonald had been a Washingtonian his entire life and that his father had been a cop, too. He'd been gunned down when he was called out to a robbery in progress at a downtown 7-Eleven.

There was a photograph at the bottom of the article of the victim and his family. Their faces smiled at me through the screen, completely unaware that out here in this timeline, one of them was dead.

Just below that was another photo. One that looked newer. I read the caption.

Family of slain DC cop at his funeral. Pictured left Sheila McDonald. Right Rahul Mc—

The caption was cut off.

I took a closer look at the photo and realized that the grown man standing next to Sheila McDonald looked awfully familiar. The image was a bit grainy and he had a black umbrella blocking half of his face from view, but I was almost certain I knew who that was.

"How is this even real?" I shot back in my chair, raising my hands to my head in complete disbelief.

This was the right badge number, only the supposed cop in the video with me wasn't the rightful owner of the badge in the first place. That cop was dead. This was an impostor who'd played cop amidst the chaos. My mind raced, connecting the dots between this impersonator and the dark chapters of Samir's murder, the protest, and Donna's murder. The ties to Jay, Rico, and Dane became clearer.

The badge and gear had been used in plain sight, though the number had likely been retired when Officer McDonald was killed. It was a symbol of honor and here his own son was dishonoring his father's name by committing crimes in his uniform. I rubbed my eyes and leaned back in, making sure that what I was seeing was actually true and not some trick of my tired mind.

But it was plain for anyone to see.

The man in the photo... *Rahul McDonald*... was Rah Meck.

CHAPTER TWENTY-NINE

COOPER
APOLOGY

An apology was more than just words. I had to show Mo that I wasn't just sorry that I got caught. How exactly I was going to do that was still beyond me, but I was determined to find a way.

I sat in the living room eating a bowl of cinnamon toast cereal when my dad came downstairs for work.

"Don't leave this house, Coop," he called out from the kitchen.

"I think I found something, Dad. Something that can help us."

"Good, you can share it with the lawyer," my dad said, heading for the front door.

"You found one yet?"

My dad stopped as he reached for the door. "You've still got time," he replied before heading out.

Even though he didn't say it, I felt that was his way of letting me know I could do what I needed to do to make things right. At least I hoped it was. Regardless, better to ask for forgiveness than permission, in this case anyway.

I had just found *the* most important piece of our investigation puzzle and I needed to relay that info to Mo ASAP, no matter what was going on between us.

I walked into the quickening heat outside and my footsteps echoed through the quiet streets. A desperate urgency propelled me to Mo's house.

When I got to her door, I reached for my phone to text her, knowing that she would have ignored my knocks.

Me: Mo, I'm outside. I know who did it!!

Mo: Don't play with me Coop

Me: forreal this time!

I waited for a reply that never came. As I grew more anxious, I frantically knocked on her door, hoping her mom had already left for work. I knocked again and heard her voice from behind the door.

"I'm getting dressed, dang! Calm down!"

She sounded just as annoyed as she had been the day before, but at least she was responsive. More importantly, she was getting dressed, which meant she was planning on opening up that door. When she did, she held it ajar—just far enough that she could peep through. Seeing her face made me all warm inside and instantly I started to feel the blood pump through my veins.

"So?" she asked. "Who is it?"

The look on her face was curious, but her eyes were tainted with caution. I took a deep breath.

"Monique, I need your help."

I hardly ever referred to her by her full name and when I did, it usually told her how serious I was. I could see that she was still grappling with the aftermath of my betrayal, but she seemed to search my eyes for sincerity. She wasn't just writing me off. She was trying to decide whether or not to trust me in that moment.

I took a step forward, breaking the distance between us, and took her hand in mine. I only hoped that she could see and feel just how sorry I was. Then I spoke softly.

"Monique, I'm so sorry for lying, for trying to be someone I'm not. I just wanted you to see me as perfect because that's how I see you. I didn't want to tell you about me being down there that day because . . ."

"What?" Mo urged, pulling her hand away from mine.

"Because I was ashamed."

My admission hung in the air. It was a confession that laid bare the insecurities I had buried and ignored since the day it happened.

"I was wrong." I sighed, reflecting on my own actions. "About looting, about so many things. I want to fight for Samir, for justice, the right way. You taught me that, Mo. Please, believe that."

Her furrowed brow softened as I spoke and bared my soul. I hoped the sincerity in my eyes could bridge the gap that betrayal had torn open. I never meant to hurt her, of all people. That's all I wanted her to know—that she was important to me and I couldn't lose her. That I valued what she thought of me more than anyone else around me.

Mo thought for a second and opened the door wider.

"Cooper, look at me."

It took all the strength I had to stare into her stern eyes without turning away out of shame.

"You have to PROMISE me. That you will never, ever lie to me again. I'm willing to give you grace, the same way I'm giving Jason grace for having that gun on him. Because I know all of this has been . . . difficult, to say the least. But if you ever give me reason to distrust you again, you'll lose me forever."

I could tell she meant it with all her heart, and there was no way I was going to do anything to push Monique Simms out of my life.

"Thank you, Mo. For real, thank you so much. I really am so sorry."

"I know you are, Coop," she said with a heavy sigh. "I can hear it in your voice and see it on your face. It's why I'm choosing to forgive you."

The huge sense of relief that I felt was like nothing else. Even with the prospect of being arrested in a matter of days—maybe hours—having Mo's forgiveness was all that mattered. The tension around us eased as Mo conceded and relaxed her shoulders. There was a silent acknowledgment of the second chance I had been granted.

"I missed you." I smiled as I leaned in for a hug and kiss.

"Oh hell nah," Mo said, turning her head away and pressing her index finger against my lips. "I forgive you, but we're going to have to build back up to that, Cooper King."

I lowered my head and blushed, embarrassed. I thought I was

slick, but I guess I wasn't slick enough to get past her defenses. I understood, though.

"Now come on in," she said, holding the door for me as I walked into the house. "We've got work to do."

I stepped in and beelined for the couch while catching Mo up on everything I'd learned in the last few hours.

"Look who the so-called cop's badge number belonged to. And look at who his son is."

I handed Mo my phone to read the article I'd found. I watched as her face turned from curiosity to horror.

"Oh my god. Coop, this is huge. I knew it! Didn't I say something wasn't right with him?"

"You did, you called it. Rah lied, while sprinkling in just enough of the truth. Donna was an undercover cop, but she never changed sides and joined his cause. She was nothing like his father."

"So Rah found out she was an undercover agent and killed her."

"Yes, but why? I can't imagine him just straight-up killing her for no reason." That part still stumped me.

"It must've had something to do with the confidential information Rah kept talking about. He said he doesn't have the files, right? What if he was actually telling the truth about that?"

I looked at Mo and nodded. It was all starting to make sense but there were still too many unanswered questions.

"We need to do something, Coop."

"I know. We have to find proof. The smoking gun. Like the badge that ties him to being at the protest. Or the murder weapon, even. Just don't know how we'd come across that."

"Oh my god," Mo muttered, her eyes popping out of her head.

"What?"

"It was right there the whole time. In plain sight."

"What are you talking about?" I asked.

"In Rah's office, there was a safe, a nice vintage piece. I thought it was decoration, but I bet that's exactly where he'd keep those things! Only problem is neither one of us know how to crack a safe."

I smirked as a thought hit me.

"Rico," I offered.

"Rico?"

"Rico knows locks, safes; he can crack anything. Besides, Rah doesn't seem like the type to be messed with. We're going to need backup."

Mo nodded, digesting my words.

"And you really think we can trust Rico?"

"He held me down, didn't give me up to you when he could've. Plus, I think he feels bad for what he's done and wants to make it right. He got his record cleared, so there's no need for him to turn on us now."

"Okay, but we need to keep a tight grip on him."

I nodded in agreement.

A sense of peace washed over me because we were a team again, but my stomach churned with anxiety. We were preparing for the last stand, and it'd be all or nothing.

CHAPTER THIRTY
COOPER
THE STING

We had come to a do-or-die moment in this whole operation and my nerves were on tenterhooks. We had assembled a lot of evidence, but without the murder weapon, our case against Rah was flimsy.

Mo seemed cool and collected, almost like she just wanted to get this over with. I kind of knew the feeling. Come what may, we were going to see this through, especially now that Pops knew about everything—plus the cops were hot on our trail.

We had spilled everything to Rico as he sat in the back of Jason's car on the way to the community center where Rah held his meetings. We'd seen online that the rally for that evening was canceled, which gave us the perfect opportunity to hit the spot while it was empty. We parked about a block away to stake the place and be sure there was no movement. Everything was quiet.

"Y'all ready to do this or what?" Mo asked, breaking the silence.

"It's what we're here for, right?" Rico said plainly, jumping out of the car.

I looked at Mo and nodded, and we followed suit. This was it. The night air hung heavy as the three of us walked stealthily through the alley behind the community center. A sense of nervous anticipation bubbled inside me, exacerbated by our large shadows that clung to the passing buildings. My breath was suspended in the unusually chilly night air as we reached the backdoor.

"You know," Rico whispered, "I wasn't expecting this from the videos you showed me. This place doesn't exactly scream struggle."

"That's because he's deluded himself into thinking that he wants what's best for DC. But all he wants is revenge," I replied.

"Let's keep the chatter to a minimum," Mo whispered back to us.

We both nodded.

"We need to be quick and quiet. Get in, get the evidence we need, and get out."

Rico threw on some leather black gloves and stepped up to pick the lock. I scanned the alley, shaking my head at the irony. This was exactly how this all had started, and after everything we'd been through, somehow, I was back to being the lookout for a B&E.

Click . . .

"We're in," Rico announced. He yanked open the door as we turned on our flashlights and stepped into the dark space.

Our senses were attuned to the smallest of noises, our ears prickling and heads swiveling with every creak and crackle.

Coming in through the back was slightly disorienting. We twisted down a few unfamiliar hallways, making our way to the main room where Rah's meetings were held. In the empty space, the room seemed much larger than before, the stage much more prominent.

"Okay, his office is just on the other side of the room," Mo whispered as she led the way.

The air seemed to thicken with every step I took. I was fully aware of the fact that he had the legal right to shoot us on sight if we were caught breaking and entering. Not that he had any concern for the law.

What's more, he probably had enough weapons to plant on us so that he could claim self-defense. Look what he'd done to Jason.

My heart was thumping in my chest. I was already on the verge of a prison sentence for a crime I hadn't committed. The last thing I needed was to have another false crime pinned on me.

Mo opened the door to Rah's office, and we were back in the lion's den.

The space was neater than the last time we'd been there. I flashed my light on the walls to get my bearings and noticed a photo I hadn't seen before. A blown-up image that echoed the one I had found online—Rah with his parents. The expensive frame housed a frozen moment of a seemingly happy family, but the dust coating the glass hinted at the dirty reality.

CRASH!

I spun to Mo and Rico.

"My bad," Rico whispered, picking up the books he'd knocked off Rah's desk.

"Never mind that," Mo hissed. "Get over here."

I followed Rico as he made his way to the corner of the room where the safe stood.

"Oof, this might take some time." Rico exhaled out as he examined the safe.

His fingers tracing the edges of the safe door made me feel like we were elegant art thieves going after some treasure, which couldn't be further from the truth. But then again, freedom is more valuable than anything.

My gaze intensified. "We need to see what's inside."

"Don't worry, I got it," Rico said, pulling out what looked like a tiny barber's bag. It wasn't. It was a pouch with even more picks. They were of all shapes and sizes. Then, he whipped out a stethoscope.

"Ayo, where'd you get that from?" I couldn't help but laugh, even in the intensity of the moment.

"You know what I went to jail for, right? Best lock pick in the whole DMV."

Rico went to work while Mo and I waited patiently. He pressed the stethoscope up against the safe and carefully worked on each rotation. With each click, a second passed. And with each passing second, the threat of someone catching us become more real. I started to sweat.

"Come on, Rico," I urged, watching the ticking clock on the wall.

"You . . . can't . . . rush . . . greatness."

Finally, after what seemed like hours, we heard a whizzing sound and one final *ping*.

"You can do the honors, ma'am," Rico said, taking a proud bow as he moved out of the way for Mo to pry the door open.

With one heave, the large steel door was opened and we had hit the motherload. Inside the safe lay the tangible evidence we sought and more: Rah's badge—or, as we knew, his father's. His entire police uniform, complete with the pistol he'd dropped when I bumped into him. Getting a clear view of it now, it looked exactly like the same type of pistol Rico had handed Jason.

"Y'all, I think this is the murder weapon!" Rico exclaimed.

We couldn't help but cheer. We'd actually done it!

Relief flooded me. I was saved. And so was Jason. But before the celebration got too out of hand, my eye spotted a folder labeled CLASSIFIED.

I reached over Mo's shoulder to collect the folder, trembling with anticipation and raw fear. I quickly skimmed through and was almost stunned speechless.

"Emails, contracts, memos . . . it's all here," I said, staring at the files.

I couldn't believe what we had stumbled on. The revelations spilled out, painting a damning portrait of corruption that reached the highest echelons of power in DC. Corruption that mostly affected DC's poor, predominantly Black residents.

"This is . . . ," Mo said in disbelief. "It's beyond anything we imagined."

As we processed the magnitude of the information in our hands, the door creaked open, shattering the moment of contemplation. A dark silhouette stood in the dimly lit room.

"Surprised to see me, kids?" Rah said.

My blood ran cold.

CHAPTER THIRTY-ONE

COOPER
FACE-OFF

The air in the room grew thick with tension as we all stared directly at Rah. I moved to position myself between him and Mo, but she stepped forward.

"It was all a lie?" she uttered so softly she could barely be heard.

Rah didn't flinch a muscle. He just rubbed his temple and looked at the sea of incriminating documents that spoke of the city's darkest secrets. His eyes darted between all three of us. It looked like he was sizing us up, calculating which one of us would be the easiest to take down first. Or maybe he was looking for a diversion so that he could get away.

"Not *all* a lie." Rah gestured to the folder in my hand. "But you've probably already read that much."

Mo looked back at the folder in my hand.

"Or have I come back too early? Want me to turn around and give you more time to ransack my home and invade my privacy?"

A solemn pause filled the room as we all waited for Rah to unravel the intricate tapestry of deception he had woven.

"Cut it out!" I yelled. "You killed Donna. You killed a Black woman you claim our community needs to protect."

"Donna only has herself to blame!" he yelled back. "She turned on me, on us, and everything we believe in right when we were about to succeed. Together."

"There never was an *us*. This was about *you*," I said sharply.

"You're shortsighted! You have no idea what you're talking about," Rah shouted as he stepped in the room and closed the door behind him. He was bigger than I remember, but maybe that's because we were standing in such a small space. Or maybe because I was starting to size him up the way he was doing with us.

"Let me tell you a story," he continued. "My father was a cop. A good one. He actually cared about the people he served. He actually considered himself a servant. And even then, when police got a bad rap, he stood on what he believed. That all cops weren't bad. Yada yada ya. Until one day, much like Donna, he witnessed his white partner kill a Black kid. He was shook because he knew the shooting wasn't justified. Yet he watched a corrupt police force paint the kid as a villain and the cop a hero. So then, he started to collect info, little by little, with plans to expose exactly what was happening."

"But he was killed during a robbery," I spoke up as it all started to click for me.

"Yes, that's what they said. But do you know there wasn't even a robbery in progress? All staged to take my father out, because they were on to what he was doing," Rah said, eerily calm.

"His last words to me were, '*We have to be our own revolutionaries. Can't wait on anybody else.*' They stuck with me, and my mission began. I've been finishing what my father started. Collecting evidence to position BLU in a way that could bring about real change. I truly thought Donna wanted to be a part of that mission. But she played me. She was a pawn, but she played me nonetheless. Leaning on the empathy I had for someone in her situation, that my father went through the same thing. In any case, I let her get close. Too close. And she stole every single piece of evidence I'd collected. I had to get it back. And I needed to silence her. She knew too much."

Another piece fell into place for me. "At her house that day, you were the masked man. You were looking for those files."

Rah nodded. "Yes, but you two interrupted me. I didn't stick around to see if others would come sniffing around, so I didn't get them then. But I went back recently and found them. And now it's time to begin the next phase of BLU. Once this hits the news, Donna will be no more than an old memory."

"It was you who contacted me," Rico cut in. "I recognize your voice. You tricked me!"

"Sorry, youngblood. Next time, hold your man down. You made it too easy. With Jason carrying the weapon it was a done deal."

Rah was filling in all the missing pieces for us. Except one.

"But why Jason?" I asked, trying to complete the picture that was being painted.

Rah looked at me with empty eyes that made my skin crawl. His expression was cold and calculating. Before he even spoke, I could tell he had no love for Jason.

"Donna infiltrated BLU through Jason, even after I told him and everybody else to be extremely careful about who we invited in. He was blinded by lust. No room for that in the revolution. With their connection, he made the perfect patsy."

"You piece of—" Mo said, lunging at Rah. I reached out to stop her just in time.

But Rah didn't flinch, instead he stoically announced, "The revolution will require sacrifices, young sister."

I looked over to Rico, who was posted by the safe. I followed his eyes to the gun that was still neatly tucked in the safe beside the police uniform.

"You can just let us go, you know," I said, taking a step toward Rah, distracting him from Mo and Rico. "You have your evidence. We believe in your cause. We're with you. We just want Jason free."

"That's going to be hard to do without giving the police another shooter. One of their own was killed. Somebody has to go down for it."

"Maybe there's another way? There's always another way," I said calmly, taking a step forward.

"I'm afraid not, young brother. Take another step, and you'll be first," Rah said, removing his hand from inside his coat to reveal the shiny muzzle of a 9mm.

Mo gasped. I wanted to run, but I couldn't even if I tried. My feet were frozen in place and my mind wasn't communicating with any of my other body parts. I was staring down the barrel of a gun held by a killer and there was nothing I could do to stop him.

First, I thought about my mom. How she was probably watching from a different realm, more terrified than she had ever been in this one. Then I thought of my dad and how crushed he'd be if I left him. And then I thought of Mo, and how I had brought her into danger.

"Please . . ." was all I could mutter. When suddenly—

"AHHHHHHHHH!" Rico yelled, followed by the clicking of an empty gun. He had grabbed the pistol from the safe and was squeezing the trigger. But no shot went off. You could see the terrifying shock land on his face when he realized the gun wasn't loaded.

Rah just shook his head.

"That one's empty. But this one isn't."

Suddenly Rah turned his arm to Rico and I'm not sure what came over me, but I seized the opportunity, jumped out, and ambushed Rah, catching him totally off guard.

It was on.

The room descended into chaos as a struggle went down. I grappled with Rah on the cold, hard floor, trying to reach the pistol he'd dropped. He was strong but his hot breath against my face told me he wouldn't be able to match my stamina. I could hear Mo's anxious shouts somewhere in the distance, but in that moment, it was just Rah and me, locked in.

Suddenly, a blur of motion caught the corner of my eye. Rico!

With a swift, precise movement, he kicked, sending Rah's pistol skittering away into the darkness of the room. A fleeting sense of triumph washed over me, but it was short-lived. Rah's powerful hands gripped me tighter, and with a ferocious yell, he threw me off him. I hit the ground hard, the air whooshing out of my lungs.

Rah was on his feet in an instant, and when I tried to rise, he kicked me hard in my stomach, completely destroying any chance I had of making it to my feet.

"Come on, tough guy," I heard him say to Rico. My lungs were burning as I tried to regain my breath from having the wind knocked out of me. Out the corner of my eyes, I could see the two exchanging a few hands, until Rah blocked Rico's right hook and hit him with a nasty uppercut. Rico toppled over.

With a swift, almost graceful movement, Rah lunged for his weapon, his fingers closing around the handle as Rico stood to his feet in front of him.

I forced myself up, ignoring the screaming pain from my ribs, the world a dizzying swirl of motion. "Rico!" I shouted, my voice hoarse with fear and exertion.

But it was too late. Rah stood before us, weapon in hand, and fired a shot. Time seemed to slow down, like the bullet was moving through water instead of air.

Then it sped up again and the bullet caught Rico in his upper body.

"NOOOOO!" Mo shouted.

Rah turned his attention to her. In that moment, I was prepared to lose my life. I needed to protect Mo at all costs. I took the deepest breath I could and willed myself.

Let's go, Coop.

And as I lunged to push Mo out of the way—

THUD!

"MPD! EVERYONE ON THE GROUND! NOW!"

Rah turned to the detectives bursting through the door.

"ON THE GROUND WE SAID!"

Rah stood there for a second, like he was weighing his next move.

And just when I thought he might shoot at the cop, he dropped his weapon, threw up his hands, and got down on the floor.

I raised my hands for Detectives Hunter and Martin to see, and Mo did the same. Turns out the card they gave me came in handy. I was able to leave word for her that Rah was the killer and we were going to confront him, and that she should meet us there if she wanted to save his life. It was dramatic, but I needed them to show up, in case things got sticky.

"Rahul McDonald, you're under arrest for the murder of Agent Donna Brown," Detective Hunter said as Martin handcuffed Rah. "You have the right to remain silent. Anything you say can and will be used against you in a court of law. You have the right to an attorney. If you cannot afford an attorney, one will be provided for you."

"You have no idea what you've done," Rah snarled, giving me the coldest stare I've ever seen. "This isn't over!" he shouted as Detective Martin led him out the door.

Already other officers were tending to Rico.

"Is Rico going to be okay?" I asked Hunter.

"It's a flesh wound, he'll be fine. *You*, on the other hand, have some explaining to do. When I got your message, I almost thought it was a prank. What would possess you to come down here alone? It wasn't smart."

I looked at Mo and she looked back, her eyes encouraging me to do what was right.

"I . . . I have a confession to make. I lied before. I *was* at the protest with Jason," I uttered, picking at my lucky bracelet. "That's how I knew he was innocent. But without proof, there's no way you would've believed me. We needed the murder weapon."

Detective Hunter just nodded her head and rubbed her chin.

"I appreciate your honesty, Coop. You saved the day. But never, under any circumstances, do something like this again. Understand?"

"Trust me, I don't plan to."

"Good. Come on, let me give y'all a ride home, I'm sure your parents are worried sick about you. We can complete the paperwork in the a.m."

Mo and I got up and followed the detective out. But before we did, I tapped my stomach, checking on the classified files I managed to hide under my shirt.

CHAPTER THIRTY-TWO

COOPER
EPILOGUE

Back on the block, things had returned to a somewhat normal state. Jason and Dane had been released and were back to kicking it in Jay's basement.

The news of Rah being arrested sent shock waves through the city because his followers were so distraught. Half of them supported what he did and the other half saw him for the maniac he was. I knew which side I stood on.

Not too long after the news of Rah broke, the mayor announced there was going to be a thorough investigation of the MPD. I just hoped it wasn't more fluff.

Knock, knock, knock . . .

I rapped on Jay's basement door, hoping he was home. He opened up with a huge grin on his face.

"My boy! Come on in, we were just about to play some 2K."

"I can't," I said shyly. "I actually was coming by because I had a question for you."

Jay stepped out of the basement and closed the door behind him.

"Of course, anything for you, Coop. What's up?"

Appreciation and an unspoken understanding floated between us, but there was something else on my mind.

"I'm going to come straight out with it. Can I . . . would you mind if I date Mo?" I asked with a mix of nerves and earnestness in my voice.

Jason stared at me for a second before he chuckled. "I can't give you permission, homie, only she can. But if it matters, you've got my blessing."

A huge grin broke out on my face. "Appreciate it, Jay."

"Of course. I owe you my life. Seriously, homie. But know, that's still baby sis."

I understood exactly what he was saying.

"You ready?" Mo's voice rang from the top of the stairs.

I looked up at her, and she was glowing, even out of the sunlight. All the weight and stress of the case seemed to have fallen off her and she looked brighter than ever. After everything we'd been through and how Mo had handled herself, I admired her even more now than I had before. It was time to put the final button on this thing.

"Yep, I'm ready," I said, shaking off my awe.

Mo and I took the train over to a local journalist at the *Washington Post*. We figured it'd be better than giving the information to the cops. No telling who we could trust over there.

Their headquarters was in a big glass building downtown. We sat across from a petite journalist, a Black woman named

Brittany. I reached in my bookbag and pulled out a manila envelope, the weight of the evidence heavy in my hands. Nervousness prickled beneath my skin but I looked to Mo, and she nodded. "I assure you, Cooper," Brittany said, "both of your names will remain anonymous, if you prefer. I'll take all the credit for this."

Mo and I cracked a smile.

"By all means," Mo said.

After one last pause, I slid the folder across the desk. Brittany picked it up. "If everything you told me over the phone is true, we're going to change the city with this story. What you all have done is beyond brave and quite honestly, I'm astounded you pulled it off. Y'all have a real future in investigative journalism."

I didn't know how true it was but it sounded good. Even made me feel a little better.

"Thanks, ma'am," I said.

"Anything else?" she inquired.

I thought for a second and shook my head as I stood up to leave.

"What are you passionate about, Cooper?" she asked.

The question caught me off guard. But not like it once had.

"I want to make a difference. I want to have an impact on my community," I said confidently. "I think we both do." I turned to Mo, who was beaming.

"Well, you're already doing it," she added, standing up. "Keep fighting the good fight."

Brittany led us back down to the lobby doors where Mo and I stepped onto a busy downtown street, surrounded by people who had no idea what we had been through. And just like that, the case was closed.

Nervous anticipation danced in the air as I waited for Mo to come back to our booth from "freshening up." We'd decided to stop and get a proper meal, something we hadn't really taken the time to do in a while. Soon as Monique returned from the restroom, the bustling noise of the outside world faded away and she was all I could concentrate on.

"So this is our first date, huh?" she asked.

"I gotta work my way back to that kiss somehow," I said, flashing a flirtatious grin.

"Well, you're off to a good start," Mo said, flirting back. "Maybe we can salvage what summer we have left."

"I'd like that."

It was just the two of us, sitting in comfortable silence as the city's pulse provided a backdrop to this new thing we were. And if that wasn't special enough, we had one hell of a story to tell of how we got here.

ACKNOWLEDGMENTS

[Text TK]